Perfect Crimes

Also by Elliott Roosevelt

Murder in the Oval Office
Murder at the Palace
The White House Pantry Murder
Murder at Hobcaw Barony
Murder in Hyde Park
Murder and the First Lady

Perfect Crimes

My Favorite Mystery Stories

•

Edited by

Elliott Roosevelt

•

St. Martin's Press New York

A · THOMAS · DUNNE · BOOK

Design by Jaye Zimet

Library of Congress Cataloging-in-Publication Data

Perfect crimes : my favorite mystery stories / edited by Elliott
    Roosevelt.
            p.   cm.
        "A Thomas Dunne book."
        ISBN 0-312-03411-3
        1. Detective and mystery stories, American.   2. Detective and
    mystery stories, English.   I. Roosevelt, Elliott, 1910—   .
    PS648.D4P47   1989   89-35321
    813'.087208—dc20   CIP

First Edition

10 9 8 7 6 5 4 3 2 1

The Order of Things

Acknowledgments

"Paper Tiger," by R. Bretnor, copyright © 1969 by R. Bretnor. Reprinted by permission of the author.

"The Nine Mile Walk," by Harry Kemelman, copyright © 1962 by Harry Kemelman. Reprinted by permission of the author and the author's agents, Scott Meredith Literary Agency, 845 Third Avenue, New York NY 10022.

"The Hands of Mr. Ottermole," by Thomas Burke, copyright © 1931, Little Brown & Co. Reprinted by permission of John Hawkins & Associates, Inc.

"Try It My Way," by Jack Ritchie, copyright © 1959 by Jack Ritchie. Reprinted by permission of the author's estate and the author's agents, Scott Meredith Literary Agency, 845 Third Avenue, New York NY 10022.

"The Two Bottles of Relish," by Lord Dunsany, from *The Little Tales of Smethers*, copyright © The estate of the late Lord Dunsany. Reproduced by permission of Curtis Brown Ltd., London.

"The Rubber Trumpet," by Roy Vickers, copyright © Roy Vickers. Reproduced by permission of Curtis Brown Ltd., London.

"One More Clue," by Craig Rice, copyright © 1965 by Craig Rice. Reprinted by permission of the author's estate and the author's agents, Scott Meredith Literary Agency, Inc., 845 Third Avenue, New York NY 10022.

"Coin of the Realm," by Stanley Ellin, copyright © Stanley Ellin. Reprinted by permission of Curtis Brown Ltd., London.

"Goodbye, Hannah," by Steve Fisher, copyright © 1938 by Steve

Introduction

This book is being compiled to save my library—or what remains of it.

Like most mystery readers, I have special favorites—and like most readers of any kind, I enjoy sharing those favorites. I have loaned out books containing these stories again and again, and gotten them back just about as often as you might think, which is not often enough.

Some of these stories were reprinted again and again, thirty or forty years ago. Recently, I haven't been seeing them. Anthologists apparently felt they'd become much too common, and went on to other works, perhaps a shade less fine than these, but surely less familiar.

The result is that these stories just aren't that familiar, not any more. Readers are coming along who simply don't know many of these classic tales, as I keep discovering when I have to loan out still another book in order to acquaint a friend with some of the best short stories ever written in the mystery or detective line.

Now, for one thing, I can stop risking valuable and elderly books; instead, I'll be able to loan out copies of this collection. Naturally, I hope I won't have to, and that my friends will all show their friendship by buying copies themselves—but I've signed and given away enough copies of my own mystery novels to have a fair idea just how over-optimistic a hope like that really is.

One way or another, though, this will certainly give readers a chance to meet the real classics in the genre, and that's the important thing, after all.

And they'll be able to do it without making further inroads on what is becoming the fastest disappearing library I know of.

—ELLIOTT ROOSEVELT

Perfect Crimes

Paper Tiger

R. Bretnor

*Ellery Queen has written that Mr. Bretnor's story
"generates almost unbearable suspense"—which it
certainly does. But I must admit that I include it here
because it may very well be the strangest political
suspense story ever written.*

*R. Bretnor is perhaps best known as a writer of
fantasy, and as the inventor of a highly complicated
sort of punning-story called (after the hero of the
stories) a Feghoot. The first Feghoots were signed
"Grendel Briarton," an anagram from which patient
readers may find out what that R. stands for.*

Loring Giroux was the direct opposite of Marshal Feng Teh-chih. There was nothing spectacular about Giroux. He had not won the Presidency of the United States by ruthlessly exterminating his rivals. He had not even campaigned for it dramatically at a time of crisis. He had inherited it. He had been a compromise Vice-President, chosen for his Southern votes and as a solid, stable counterweight to the flamboyance of Cardey Corcoran. Then, two months after Corcoran took office, to the sorrow of the ladies and the relief of many high-placed people in his own administration, Cardey had crashed his private plane into a mountainside, taking half his Cabinet along with him, and Loring Giroux had moved quietly, with his wife and one unmarried daughter, his shaggy sheepdog and his yellow cat, into the loneliest house in the world.

That was when Marshal Feng Teh-chih had started in on him.

Loring Giroux's background was as quiet and solid as his person. He had been a naval officer in the Tojo War, a junior deck officer aboard high-test tankers. He had a few decorations, awarded after forgotten actions in which nothing much had happened to his ship—twice against subs, more often against air attacks. He had served in the Louisiana State Legislature. He had been appointed to a Board or two in Washington, to something in the OAS, and then to a South American ambassadorship. Between times he had practiced law at home. Finally, he had been elected Governor, and then—to everyone's surprise—Vice-President.

Giroux's ancestry went back before the Louisiana Purchase on the one hand, and to the Revolution on the other. His grandfather had come out of the Civil War a young captain under Jubal Early; afterward he had wandered angrily into the West and Mexico, finally returning to a late marriage and a reconciliation with his country. His father had gone to West Point, and had retired, a colonel, after the obsolescence of the cavalry. Giroux himself was neither short nor tall, neither fat nor thin. His main distinguishing feature was a slightly Teddy Rooseveltish mustache, which the political cartoonists—Chinese and American alike—had latched onto immediately.

The cartoonists also—the Chinese especially, because they had been ordered to—went for the big striped yellow tomcat. American cartoonists, even the opposition, were almost kind about it: they loved to show Giroux asking the cat's advice on how to catch the mice of international politics, or how he could turn himself into Cardey Corcoran. But the Chinese used it to illustrate their ancient Paper Tiger theme. Loring Giroux, they screamed, had brought Beauregard to the White House to prove that the American paper tiger wasn't made of paper after all. The Chinese madness had made a great deal of headway since the days of Mao Tse-tung and his Red Guards, and Marshal Feng, a Red Guard graduate, had turned it to his private purposes.

Feng concentrated on President Giroux. The Russians now were seldom named, and then only as Giroux's criminal, treacherous, and unspeakable collaborators. Giroux was a weakling. Giroux was the degenerate symbol of a decadent bourgeois society. The missiles, the fusion weapons, which he as President controlled—these were the Paper Tiger. The young and vigorous Maoist Workers State, wielding its unconquerable weapon—the thoughts of Mao and of Feng Teh-chih, though Mao's were fading rather rapidly—would certainly triumph for the simple reason that survival was the natural prize awarded to the fittest.

The fittest would survive!—so proclaimed Marshal Feng. It was a curious Marxist Darwinism, naive, grossly over-simplified, trumpeted with each new insult, each new prov-ocation. It accompanied the wiping out of the Hong Kong and Macao enclaves, and the overrunning of Nepal. It became even more personal and more strident when Feng launched his invasion of North India late in the 1970's, penetrating deep into Assam.

Feng's personal attack on Loring Giroux was ridiculous. The press of the Free World thought so, and laughed about it several days a week. The press of the Neutralist and non-Chinese-Communist aligned nations took a similar, though rather self-consciously anti-American, stance. The State Department thought it was absurd; so did the Joint Chiefs of Staff. Every Security Council meeting included a few moments of innocent merriment focused on Feng's personal venom against Giroux.

Until, that is, the Council met on the 16th of September. It was a crash session, with the Joint Chiefs in attendance. Marshal Feng had gone on the air that morning, and Pres-ident Giroux opened the meeting five and a half hours later. He looked around at the faces, the uniforms, the business suits.

"Gentlemen," he said, "I know that you all have either watched Feng's latest performance or heard about it. Still, we're going to replay it, so there'll be no misunderstand-ing."

"Mr. President," exclaimed the Secretary of Defense,

4

"Feng's just a crazy thug. Aren't you taking his nonsense a little seriously?"

"A little, Jake. It isn't every day a man gets this kind of invitation. Let's watch our boy again."

He gestured them to silence, picked up translation headphones, but didn't put them on immediately. Feng appeared without warning on the screen—a tall long-faced North Chinese with basalt eyes. He was lean and hard, obviously an athlete. He turned his speech on suddenly, full blast, like turning on a fire siren.

"Who does he remind you of?" asked the President, unsmiling, knowing that no reply was necessary, that despite the difference of race, language, and doctrine the image of Hitler came instantly to every mind. The speech was Feng's usual one, an almost hysterical rodomontade using all the old clichés, but this time, after barely fifteen minutes, coming to a very different climax.

"You are a filthy Capitalist coward, Loring Giroux. You are afraid of me and of the irresistible thought of Mao Tse-tung. You are afraid because the working masses and their leaders do not fear your paper tiger. We spit on you, Giroux! You are not fit to survive. I will destroy your vile imperialism. I will humiliate you. I, Feng Teh-chih—I myself will rub your face in filth. Coward! You are afraid to fight, I challenge you to fight, to fight *me*, with your hands, with guns, with knives, anywhere, at any time, with any weapons you desire! Do you understand, Mr. President of the United States? Do you dare to fight me, Feng Teh-chih, before the world? No, you do not. You know that you could not survive, you corrupt weakling! I will show you how I will destroy you, Paper Tiger—"

On the screen an aide stepped into view, carrying a striped orange cat—a cat that looked as much like Beauregard as possible. Feng's left hand grasped it, lifted it.

5

Then with a swift and brutal judo chop he broke its back. He hurled the poor small body against a wall, showed all his teeth, and screamed, *"That* is how I kill you, weak Giroux!"

The screen went blank. The show was over. There was silence. Such a display was difficult for men used to the normal courses of diplomacy to understand. Even the Joint Chiefs, men of war, still could not quite believe what they had seen. Had it not been a replay their reaction would have been immediate. As it was, they hesitated, looked at the President questioningly, and began to simmer as the pressure rose.

Before it could erupt Giroux touched them with his voice. It was not harsh. But it was quiet as cold steel. *"Don't,"* he said. "Don't comment. That's not the purpose of this get-together."

State looked at CIA, CIA at Defense; the Joint Chiefs exchanged anxious glances.

"You are here for one reason and one reason only—" Loring Giroux rose "—to hear my decision regarding Marshal Feng's challenge. I have accepted it."

There are things which never should be dropped: rare porcelains, pots of hot molten lead, live hand grenades. People react too naturally. Instantly noise erupted. *But it's illegal for a Presi . . . Not constitu . . . Without any consultation! . . . B-but we're a civilized peo . . .*

Loring Giroux looked at Quinton, Army, who was sounding off as loudly as the rest. "General Quinton!"

Quinton stood, large and dark and graying. He put his palms flat down on the shining table, letting his jaw and football shoulders jut out over it. The others became silent.

"Mr. President," boomed Quinton. "You've flipped. You, sir, are out of your ever-loving mind."

6

"Why?" rapped Giroux.

"Because, dammit, you're sixty-one years old. You're in no shape to fight him hand to hand. Even when we were kids you couldn't learn to shoot for sour apples. Feng's in top condition. There's not a weapon he's not expert in. You're outclassed—that's why!"

"Is that all, Quinton?"

"Mr. President—Laurie—" Quinton pleaded now. "Look, you just can't *do* it. Anyhow, military law prohibits dueling, you know that. We—we'll have to stop you!"

There was noise again.

"Be *quiet!*" There was a lash of discipline in Giroux's voice. "You *cannot* stop me. My message of acceptance went out an hour ago. It is being broadcast all over the world. General Quinton, I am as expert in the weapon I have chosen as Marshall Feng can be. My physical condition is more than adequate. As for legality, we'll fight in Uruguay, where dueling's legal. Besides—"

He stopped and regarded them. "What the hell do you propose to do about it? Use violence against me? Mount a quick revolution? Don't be dammed fools. I am not only President of the United States, gentlemen. I am Commander-in-Chief of our armed forces. I have already issued orders to all those immediately concerned."

State pushed his chair back. Blood draining from his face, he stood erect. "I cannot be a party to this—this savagery, th-this absurdity. Man, can't you think what you'll be doing to this country's image everywhere? To your own? I—I *resign.*"

"Earnshaw," Giroux said, "what will Feng do to our image if I ignore him? If I refuse to fight? Don't you see —it may be I won't win, but I can't *lose.* Even if he kills me Feng can't win. And if any of you does try to stop me—if you so much as *try*—what will that do to our country's image when the news gets out? What will it do for Feng?"

He sat down slowly and deliberately. The others hesitated, weighing the chances, each trying to guess what the rest would do. Almost imperceptibly the Joint Chiefs seemed to move in a little closer to each other, to the President.

Quinton sat down. Finally, muttering, the Secretary of State lowered himself into his chair. Their heavy breathing was the only sound.

"For a long time," said the President, "something has been needed to clear the air—preferably to clear it of Feng. I'll grant you that my acceptance is a break with all tradition, with diplomatic usage, but—believe me—I know what I am doing."

"That's asking us to take a lot on faith," Quinton put in. "I'll grant you, sir, you've called your shots right in the past, but—"

"Feng and I will fight at three o'clock tomorrow afternoon. With weapons of my choosing, under conditions set by me. Exactly equal weapons and conditions for both of us, naturally. No practice will be necessary for either of us. And each of us will bring three seconds, including an interpreter."

"Who will they be, sir?" Navy asked.

Giroux smiled. "First, if he cares to come, General Quinton, who has watched me shoot. Major Harrison Ouyang, of Air-Space, who will interpret for our side. And Sergeant Easting, Sergeant Major of the Army, who holds the Congressional Medal of Honor from Vietnam and who was good enough to carry my message of acceptance to the Polish Embassy." He saw annoyance on the face of the

8

Navy. "I myself will represent our service, Admiral," he explained. "Who Feng's seconds will turn out to be, I of course do not know. That is all, gentlemen. Turn on your TV sets tomorrow. Our encounter will probably get worldwide coverage, live."

"Or dead," the Secretary of State said through his teeth.

"Or dead," the President agreed. He rose and made a gesture of dismissal. They filed out, strangely silent, and politely the President walked them to the door.

Quinton, last to leave, held back a little. "How'd I do?" he whispered.

"Beautifully, Tom, beautifully." The President touched his shoulder. "Just as if you'd never heard a word about it."

"You're *still* nuts," growled Quinton.

The world press reacted—unpredictably, chaotically, often hysterically. But frequently policy was drowned in the enthusiasm of newsmen—enthusiasm for the unexpected courage, for the brave cutting of a Gordian knot, for a lost chivalry, for Giroux himself. Only rarely was there enthusiasm for Feng, and that, as *Le Monde* later pointed out, was usually of an "or else" variety.

There were solemn protests in the United Nations—protests which went round and round and ended nowhere. The temperate Scandinavians, the Dutch, the Indians and Ceylonese, the more leftish Britons disapproved—but their disapproval was usually of the principle, seldom of the man. The French, not too surprisingly, changed sides at once, recalled the duels of men like Clemenceau, and attributed Giroux's most admirable sense of personal and national honor to his Gallic ancestry. The Poles and the Hungarians, forgetting all their ties with the East, came out just as strongly. So did the Japanese. Latin America literally went wild. As for the Russians, they broadcast their denunciations almost incomprehensibly in Marxist dialectic.

The press at home was even more confusing and confused. A San Francisco newspaper perhaps outdid the rest. It ran three major editorials: one damned President Giroux as a Racist Southerner bent on National Suicide; another compared him quite favorably with Generals Andrew Jackson and MacArthur; the third, striking at the iniquities of an unfinished local rapid transit system, said flatly that no institution as evil as the duel could possibly solve problems which were sociologically insoluble.

Secretary of State Earnshaw resigned, as publicly as possible, and demanded instant emergency action by the Congress. Neither the Congress nor the press paid much attention to him. Before the subject could even be brought up in either House, Giroux was on his way—and every politician realized that in spite of any odds, he *might* come back the winner. It was no time for drastic statements, or drastic action.

Before he went to bed that night the President said goodbye to his lady. He told her that he loved her, and they remembered something thirty years gone by, something small and really unimportant and very precious only to themselves. She had guessed what he planned to do.

He kissed her, and she asked, "How—how are you going to fight him, Loring?"

He looked away from her. "The way Cousin Kerby fought the steamboat man."

"I was afraid of that," she whispered, remembering all the details of that duel a century and a quarter in the past, when Kerby Loring and the steamboat man had met each other on the Mississippi. "Yes, I was afraid of that."

Then, to make things easier, the President said, very

softly, "Goodbye, Jen," and kissed her through her tears, and quickly went away.

The next day, when his plane set down at Montevideo Airport, Giroux seemed fresh and rested, though some observers thought they saw signs of strain around his mouth. He met a hero's welcome. The President of Uruguay was an old fishing and poker-playing friend, from OAS days; before either of them had become a President they had exchanged visits in each other's houses, in each other's countries. Besides, Fernando Estrada Orde had himself fought a duel or two, with sabers, once against a Uruguayan colonel, again with a combative professor-journalist. Now, under his properly sober brows, his eyes were flashing, aware of the personal drama his friend was facing, the unprecedented history which would soon be made. They walked together to the waiting limousines, under the guns of four armored cars.

"Feng is here," Estrada said, when they were under way. "He arrived less than an hour ago. I have given him an unusually heavy escort." He smiled, showing his strong teeth. "I almost hope he violates our hospitality. I do not like the man."

"All the arrangements have been made?" Giroux asked, in Spanish.

"*Sí*. My military aide went out this morning, with the North Korean minister and some sort of delegate from Peking, and they bought the ammunition and the guns. My aide did not choose the shops; they did. They bought four guns, as you requested—in four separate places. They are being very careful."

"*Naturalmente*. And the rest?"

"As you specified. Feng has been shown your requirements. He has agreed to meet you in an empty office in

11

our Ministry of Agriculture, where there is room for TV cameras. From there you and he will go into the other room, where all is as you wanted it, but that room he does not know about."

"Otherwise he is satisfied?"

"*De seguro*. He says that he can kill you anywhere."

There was a silence before Estrada asked, "How do you propose to fight this man, my friend? Now that we have bought the tools, how will you use them?"

He listened to Giroux's explanation, then spoke very softly. "I should not say this thing to you, *amigo*. I should never say it to the head of a great and friendly state. But do you realize that you are mad?"

"How would *you* fight him?"

"I have watched him. I would never fight him unless I absolutely had to."

"I have to," said the President of the United States.

They entered the small room simultaneously, by adjoining doors, each group escorted by four Uruguayan officers. The room was new and almost bare, its slate-gray walls forbidding. Between the doors stood a table, guarded by two more Uruguayans and a grim Chinese. On it there were four double-barreled shotguns and a box of shells.

Feng was in his marshal's uniform. In the flesh he seemed even taller, harder, straighter than on the television screen. His cold eyes had taken in the room; obviously he did not like what he had seen. He was speaking to one of his three seconds who, like Quinton and Ouyang and Sergeant Easting, were armed with submachine guns. Feng's seconds were burly men, obviously military but with more than a hint of secret police about them. Loring Giroux was the only man there out of uniform; he wore slacks and a tweed jacket.

12

"Sir, he's been asking whether he's on TV," Major Ou-yang said, *sotto voce*. "They've told him he is, and he's annoyed because there's just one camera. It looks like he's going to make a speech."

Almost immediately the lights went on dazzlingly, and the familiar tirade started.

"Want me to translate it, sir? It's the same malarkey, only he's accusing you of trickery. He says he's going to kill you anyhow."

"Don't bother," Loring Giroux answered. "I've heard it all before." He watched Feng's mobile face, and listened to the ranting voice, and wondered if he had underestimated him, or overestimated him, or—Abruptly in his mind he saw a picture of Ouyang, of his expression when he had looked at Feng. Ouyang's parents, he recalled, had been in China when the Reds took over.

"Major—" he smiled at him "—let's try and keep it cool, shall we?"

As suddenly as it had started the speech was over, and Feng was barking questions.

"Sir, he wants to know just what the conditions are."

"Tell him," said the President, speaking very clearly, "that we are going to fight with two of those four shotguns. Remind him that they were chosen by his own people, not by ours, and that there was no time for prearrangement or collusion. Tell him to pick two guns—any two—then select one of the two for himself. I will take one of the two remaining."

They waited while the Marshal and his seconds made a choice. Then Giroux made his. He picked a double-trigger brush gun, with 25-inch barrels, by Francotte, opened it, checked the safety, locks, and firing pins.

"Now, Mr. President, this Feng demands to know where you will fight."

"Say that I will tell him after we enter the next room. We will go first."

They went through the door, which a Uruguayan brigadier opened for them; then, carefully and suspiciously, Feng and his seconds followed them. It was a room slightly larger than the other, windowless, equally slate-gray. It was glaringly illuminated for the TV cameras which, raised on platforms high above the floor, stared down through armor plate. Dead center there was a standard poker table, with two facing chairs. An armor screen was so placed that the seconds, three on each side of the screen, would hold the table in their field of fire—but would not be able to fire at each other.

"What does this mean?" demanded Feng.

"Tell him," Giroux said. "It means that we will fight here, in this room. Tell him that in my part of the United States, many years ago, we had a type of duel which men fought only when nothing else could settle a dispute— when neither would be satisfied with less. We will sit together at that poker table he and I. Face to face we will aim our loaded shotguns at each other, our fingers on the triggers. Then we will wait while the countdown clock—" he pointed at the wall "—ticks off one minute. The last ten seconds of the countdown will be oral, spoken aloud. When it comes to zero we will fire—together. If either of us fires prematurely, the other's seconds will be free to kill him. It is all very simple."

Feng listened to his interpreter's translation, and as he listened his brows drew together like gathering thunderclouds. His voice erupted in a burst of rage.

Loring Giroux waited for no translation. "Ask him," he said. "Is he afraid?"

Ouyang snapped out a few contemptuous words of Mandarin. There was no answer. Momentarily a look of cal-

14

culation flickered across the anger on Feng's face. Then, spitting on the floor viciously, he strode toward the table in the center of the room.

Briefly, after that, politeness and formality took over. Two Uruguayan field officers stood behind each chair. They bowed to the two duelists. They seated them. They ushered the two groups of seconds into their positions, the Americans with their Smith & Wesson 9mm caseless submachine guns on one side of the impenetrable screen, the Chinese with their approximately equal pieces on the other. Then the Uruguayan field officers left the room, closing the door behind them.

The brigadier stepped forward. "Gentlemen," he asked, "are you ready?"

Loring Giroux, looking into the twin muzzles of Feng's gun, said, "I am ready."

Feng nodded.

The brigadier stepped back out of the seconds' field of fire. "Begin!" he ordered.

The countdown clock began to tick. Like every fatal, final clock it ticked with an immense and deadly slowness.

Sixty.

Fifty-nine.

Fifty-eight.

While the world held its breath Loring Giroux raised his eyes to the unfamiliar and unfathomed eyes confronting him. He had done this at many another poker table, not always at completely friendly games. But it had never been like this. He felt the mounting tension, the silent-screaming tautness of friends and enemies.

Fifty-six.

Fifty-five.

Fifty-

Strangely, his own tenseness did not mount. He knew

15

he was afraid, but it was as though he rode his fear with tightly gathered reins. Looking into those eyes, into their blackness, he thought, *Did I read him right? Have I succeeded in reading him at all? What sort of hand does he think he's holding? What does he make of me? Now that he knows what this is all about, how is he really taking it? He must have thought he had it all figured out just now when he decided to shut up and fight. Did I judge him right?*

The clock ticked on, but Loring Giroux made no attempt to keep count. Perhaps forty seconds were left—forty or thirty-eight or thirty-seven. It made no difference—in less than a minute he faced certain death. *Here!* He brought himself up short. *Now that's no way to think.* He saw the cable-tightness of Feng's jaw, and wondered if Feng also felt fear. *This is how the world stands today,* he thought. *That is why he and I must kill each other—*

Suddenly his fear welled up within him, and the outcome, whose certainty he had not fully dared to face, confronted him, and through his mind flowed all those thoughts which come to men who know they are about to die. Thoughts of those loved, those lost, those who would never touch his hand again. He tried to tell himself that even though he died his country could not lose. Nor could the world. Feng could not win.

Oh, God! Were there now only twenty seconds between him and death? Twenty? Perhaps only fifteen.

He dropped his eyes. He saw the fingers of Marshal Feng's left hand, around the fore end of the pointed gun. Five precious seconds passed before he comprehended their significance. Their knuckles were beginning to turn white, and on the index finger's tip stood one small drop of sweat. And there was one thing more.

16

Then his own fear fell away. He raised his eyes again and looked once more into the eyes of Feng Teh-chih, and smiled.

"Ten!" called the Uruguayan brigadier.

Slowly, with the ticking clock, the brigadier counted down, while the Marshal and the President measured the death that lay between them. His voice rising against his will, the brigadier said,

"Six."

"Five."

"Four."

And with three seconds left Feng very deliberately put his shotgun on the table and stood up.

It was an excellent performance. Feng's face, carefully composed, showed only anger and contempt. Even his voice, at first, was thoroughly controlled. "This is an idiocy!" he said. "Did you think that I, Feng Teh-chih, would really sit and play your stupid game?" Then suddenly he yelled, "It can prove nothing, nothing, *nothing*! I shall not let the Chinese people be cheated by this trick of the imperialists! *Never!* I—I shall yet defeat you, weak Giroux!"

Loring Giroux, of course, did not learn what he had said until he heard it translated later—but he divined its meaning. "Well, Marshal Feng," he answered, "are you leaving us? These shotguns are as nothing compared to H-bombs. Surely you aren't going to give up so good a chance to prove that I'm a paper tiger?"

Feng did not wait for a translation. He sent his chair crashing to the floor and bellowed to his seconds. Then without another word he marched out through the door, and they followed him.

Loring Giroux knew that death left with them. Gradually

17

his fingers on the shotgun relaxed. Mechanically he opened the gun, took out the shells. He pushed his own chair back—

Then there was tumult all around him. Estrada Orde had pulled him to his feet and was embracing him. Major Ouyang was doing his best to shake his hand. Quinton, swearing mightily, was pounding him on the back. Newsmen were swarming in, and the TV crews were practically hysterical. Champagne appeared.

It was not until some hours afterward, when finally they were relaxing in the plane, that General Quinton said, "My God, that was tight there for a while. Laurie, I would've sworn that guy would never chicken out."

"He didn't," said the President.

"Sir?"

"He didn't. He's no coward. He's just completely practical; he'd never give his life unless he'd win by doing it —undying fame, perhaps. At least a victory. He had me buffaloed for just a minute though—until I saw his hands. He wasn't keyed up half enough—not for a man who'd put on all those raving acts. His hands were tight, but they weren't tight enough, and they were steady as a rock. It was then I knew he wouldn't go the route, that he was waiting for *me* to back down. He's not a good poker player."

"What about the threat he'd defeat you later?"

"That was for the home folks. Now he's going to try and play another hand. He figures he'll get it all explained away, or if not, he'll simply polish off the opposition. But this time I think he's wrong. I think he's done for. His people don't like losers."

Two weeks later, Loring Giroux dismissed a special evening meeting of his Cabinet and went upstairs to where his wife was waiting. He scratched the sheepdog sitting by the

18

desk. He rubbed Beauregard's smug whiskers. "That cat's getting fatter than a pig," he said. "What have you been feeding him?"

She smiled. "Shrimp, liver, and filet mignon."

"He has it coming. He's no paper tiger." He returned her smile. "You've heard the news?"

"Feng?"

"Yes, he's down the drain. But, Jen, that isn't all. The Chinese have just sent a message to the world. They want no across-the-table shotgun duels; they said exactly that. They want to settle all outstanding differences. It's just been broadcast."

She came to him, took his hands, and kissed him on the lips. "Oh, God!" she whispered. "The way Cousin Kerby fought the steamboat man—oh, thank God!"

Then Loring Giroux put his arm around her and led her to the doors that gave out on the balcony and threw the doors open.

They stood there together, breathing the clear new air.

The Nine Mile Walk

Harry Kemelman

Harry Kemelman is best known for his novels about
Rabbi Small, the series which began with the
wonderful Friday the Rabbi Slept Late. *He's also the
author of one of the classic pure-deduction stories, and
here it is.*

*Nicky Welt, who stars in this stunner, is also a series
character—the collection of short stories (also called*
The Nine Mile Walk) *by Mr. Kemelman contains
several other, almost equally startling, adventures.*

I had made an ass of myself in a speech I had given at the Good Government Association dinner, and Nicky Welt had cornered me at breakfast at the Blue Moon, where we both ate occasionally, for the pleasure of rubbing it in. I had made the mistake of departing from my prepared speech to criticize a statement my predecessor in the office of County Attorney had made to the press. I had drawn a number of inferences from his statement and had thus left myself open to a rebuttal which he had promptly made and which had the effect of making me appear intellectually dishonest. I was new to this political game, having but a few months before left the Law School faculty to become the Reform Party candidate for County Attorney. I said as much in extenuation, but Nicholas Welt, who could never drop his pedagogical manner (he was Snowdon Professor of English Language and Literature), replied in much the same tone that he would dismiss a request from a sophomore for an extension on a term paper, "That's no excuse."

Although he is only two or three years older than I, in his late forties, he always treats me like a schoolmaster hectoring a stupid pupil. And I, perhaps because he looks so much older with his white hair and lined, gnomelike face, suffer it.

"They were perfectly logical inferences," I pleaded.

"My dear boy," he purred, "although human intercourse is well-nigh impossible without inference, most inferences

22

are usually wrong. The percentage of error is particularly high in the legal profession where the intention is not to discover what the speaker wishes to convey, but rather what he wishes to conceal."

I picked up my check and eased out from behind the table.

"I suppose you are referring to cross-examination of witnesses in court. Well, there's always an opposing counsel who will object if the inference is illogical."

"Who said anything about logic?" he retorted. "An inference can be logical and still not be true."

He followed me down the aisle to the cashier's booth. I paid my check and waited impatiently while he searched in an old-fashioned change purse, fishing out coins one by one and placing them on the counter beside his check, only to discover that the total was insufficient. He slid them back into his purse and with a tiny sigh extracted a bill from another compartment of the purse and handed it to the cashier.

"Give me any sentence of ten or twelve words," he said, "and I'll build you a logical chain of inferences that you never dreamed of when you framed the sentence."

Other customers were coming in, and since the space in front of the cashier's booth was small, I decided to wait outside until Nicky completed his transaction with the cashier. I remember being mildly amused at the idea that he probably thought I was still at his elbow and was going right ahead with his discourse.

When he joined me on the sidewalk I said, "A nine mile walk is no joke, especially in the rain."

"No, I shouldn't think it would be," he agreed absently. Then he stopped in his stride and looked at me sharply. "What the devil are you talking about?"

"It's a sentence and it has eleven words," I insisted.

And I repeated the sentence, ticking off the words on my fingers.

"What about it?"

"You said that given a sentence of ten or twelve words—"

"Oh, yes." He looked at me suspiciously. "Where did you get it?"

"It just popped into my head. Come on now, build your inferences."

"You're serious about this?" he asked, his little blue eyes glittering with amusement. "You really want me to?"

It was just like him to issue a challenge and then to appear amused when I accepted it. And it made me angry.

"Put up or shut up," I said.

"All right," he said mildly. "No need to be huffy. I'll play. Hm-m, let me see, how did the sentence go? 'A nine mile walk is no joke, especially in the rain.' Not much to go on there."

"It's more than ten words," I rejoined.

"Very well." His voice became crisp as he mentally squared off to the problem. "First inference: the speaker is aggrieved."

"I'll grant that," I said, "although it hardly seems to be an inference. It's really implicit in the statement."

He nodded impatiently. "Next inference: the rain was unforeseen, otherwise he would have said, 'A nine mile walk in the rain is no joke,' instead of using the 'especially' phrase as an afterthought."

"I'll allow that," I said, "although it's pretty obvious."

"First inferences should be obvious," said Nicky tartly.

I let it go at that. He seemed to be floundering and I didn't want to rub it in.

"Next inference: the speaker is not an athlete or an outdoors man."

24

"You'll have to explain that one," I said.

"It's the 'especially' phrase again," he said. "The speaker does not say that a nine mile walk in the rain is no joke, but merely the walk—just the distance, mind you—is no joke. Now, nine miles is not such a terribly long distance. You walk more than half that in eighteen holes of golf—and golf is an old man's game," he added slyly. *I* play golf.

"Well, that would be all right under ordinary circumstances," I said, "but there are other possibilities. The speaker might be a soldier in the jungle, in which case nine miles would be a pretty good hike, rain or no rain."

"Yes," and Nicky was sarcastic, "and the speaker might be one-legged. For that matter, the speaker might be a graduate student writing a Ph.D. thesis on humor and starting by listing all the things that are not funny. See here, I'll have to make a couple of assumptions before I continue."

"How do you mean?" I asked, suspiciously.

"Remember, I'm taking this sentence *in vacuo*, as it were. I don't know who said it or what the occasion was. Normally a sentence belongs in the framework of a situation."

"I see. What assumptions do you want to make?"

"For one thing, I want to assume that the intention was not frivolous, that the speaker is referring to a walk that was actually taken, and that the purpose of the walk was not to win a bet or something of that sort."

"That seems reasonable enough," I said.

"And I also want to assume that the locale of the walk is here."

"You mean here in Fairfield?"

"Not necessarily. I mean in this general section of the country."

"Fair enough."

"Then, if you grant those assumptions, you'll have to accept my last inference that the speaker is no athlete or outdoors man."

"Well, all right, go on."

"Then my next inference is that the walk was taken very late at night or very early in the morning—say, between midnight and five or six in the morning."

"How do you figure that one?" I asked.

"Consider the distance, nine miles. We're in a fairly well-populated section. Take any road and you'll find a community of some sort in less than nine miles. Hadley is five miles away, Hadley Falls is seven and a half, Goreton is eleven, but East Goreton is only eight and you strike East Goreton before you come to Goreton. There is local train service along the Goreton road and bus service along the others. All the highways are pretty well traveled. Would anyone have to walk nine miles in a rain unless it were late at night when no buses or trains were running and when the few automobiles that were out would hesitate to pick up a stranger on the highway?"

"He might not have wanted to be seen," I suggested.

Nicky smiled pityingly. "You think he would be less noticeable trudging along the highway than he would be riding in a public conveyance where everyone is usually absorbed in his newspaper?"

"Well, I won't press the point," I said brusquely.

"Then try this one: he was walking toward a town rather than away from one."

I nodded. "It is more likely, I suppose. If he were in a town, he could probably arrange for some sort of transportation. Is that the basis for your inference?"

"Partly that," said Nicky, "but there is also an inference

26

to be drawn from the distance. Remember, it's a *nine* mile walk and nine is out of the exact numbers."

"I'm afraid I don't understand."

That exasperated schoolteacher-look appeared on Nicky's face again. "Suppose you say, 'I took a ten mile walk' or 'a hundred mile drive'; I would assume that you actually walked anywhere from eight to a dozen miles, or that you rode between ninety and a hundred and ten miles. In other words, *ten* and *hundred* are round numbers. You might have walked *exactly* ten miles or just as likely you might have walked *approximately* ten miles. But when you speak of walking *nine* miles, I have a right to assume that you have named an exact figure. Now, we are far more likely to know the distance of the city from a given point than we are to know the distance of a given point from the city. That is, ask anyone in the city how far out Farmer Brown lives, and if he knows him, he will say, 'Three or four miles.' But ask Farmer Brown how far he lives from the city and he will tell you. 'Three and six-tenths miles— measured it on my speedometer many a time.' "

"It's weak, Nicky," I said.

"But in conjunction with your own suggestion that he could have arranged transportation if he had been in a city—"

"Yes, that would do it," I said. "I'll pass it. Any more?"

"I've just begun to hit my stride," he boasted. "My next inference is that he was going to a definite destination and that he had to be there at a particular time. It was not a case of going off to get help because his car broke down or his wife was going to have a baby or somebody was trying to break into his house."

"Oh, come now," I said, "the car breaking down is really the most likely situation. He could have known the exact

27

distance from having checked the mileage just as he was leaving the town."

Nicky shook his head. "Rather than walk nine miles in the rain, he would have curled up on the back seat and gone to sleep, or at least stayed by his car and tried to flag another motorist. Remember, it's nine miles. What would be the least it would take him to hike it?"

"Four hours," I offered.

He nodded. "Certainly no less, considering the rain. We've agreed that it happened very late at night or very early in the morning. Suppose he had his breakdown at one o'clock in the morning. It would be five o'clock before he would arrive. That's daybreak. You begin to see a lot of cars on the road. The buses start just a little later. In fact, the first buses hit Fairfield around five-thirty. Besides, it he were going for help, he would not have to go all the way to town—only as far as the nearest telephone. No, he had a definite appointment, and it was in a town, and it was for some time before five-thirty."

"Then why couldn't he have got there earlier and waited?" I asked. "He could have taken the last bus, arrived around one o'clock, and waited until his appointment. He walks nine miles in the rain instead, and you said he was no athlete."

We had arrived at the Municipal Building where my office is. Normally, any arguments begun at the Blue Moon ended at the entrance to the Municipal Building. But I was interested in Nicky's demonstration and I suggested that he come up for a few minutes.

When we were seated I said, "How about it, Nicky, why couldn't he have arrived early and waited?"

"He could have," Nicky retorted. "But since he did not, we must assume that he was either detained until after the

28

last bus left, or that he had to wait where he was for a signal of some sort, perhaps a telephone call."

"Then according to you, he had an appointment some time between midnight and five-thirty—"

"We can draw it much finer than that. Remember, it takes him four hours to walk the distance. The last bus stops at twelve-thirty A.M. If he doesn't take that, but starts at the same time, he won't arrive at his destination until four-thirty. On the other hand, if he takes the first bus in the morning, he will arrive around five-thirty. That would mean that his appointment was for some time between four-thirty and five-thirty."

"You mean that if his appointment was earlier than four-thirty, he would have taken the last night bus, and if it was later than five-thirty, he would have taken the first morning bus?"

"Precisely. And another thing: if he was waiting for a signal or a phone call, it must have come not much later than one o'clock."

"Yes, I see that," I said. "If his appointment is around five o'clock and it takes him four hours to walk the distance, he'd have to start around one."

He nodded, silent and thoughtful. For some queer reason I could not explain, I did not feel like interrupting his thoughts. On the wall was a large map of the county and I walked over to it and began to study it.

"You're right, Nicky," I remarked over my shoulder, "there's no place as far as nine miles away from Fairfield that doesn't hit another town first. Fairfield is right in the middle of a bunch of smaller towns."

He joined me at the map. "It doesn't have to be Fairfield, you know," he said quietly. "It was probably one of the outlying towns he had to reach. Try Hadley."

"Why Hadley? What would anyone want in Hadley at five o'clock in the morning?"

"The Washington Flyer stops there to take on water about that time," he said quietly.

"That's right, too," I said. "I've heard that train many a night when I couldn't sleep. I'd hear it pulling in and then a minute or two later I'd hear the clock on the Methodist Church banging out five." I went back to my desk for a timetable. "The Flyer leaves Washington at twelve forty-seven A.M. and gets into Boston at eight A.M."

Nicky was still at the map measuring distances with a pencil.

"Exactly nine miles from Hadley is the Old Sumter Inn," he announced.

"Old Sumter Inn," I echoed. "But that upsets the whole theory. You can arrange for transportation there as easily as you can in a town."

He shook his head. "The cars are kept in an enclosure and you have to get an attendant to check you through the gate. The attendant would remember anyone taking out his car at a strange hour. It's a pretty conservative place. He could have waited in his room until he got a call from Washington about someone on the Flyer—maybe the number of the car and the berth. Then he could just slip out of the hotel and walk to Hadley."

I stared at him, hypnotized.

"It wouldn't be difficult to slip aboard while the train was taking on water, and then if he knew the car number and the berth—"

"Nicky," I said portentously, "as the Reform District Attorney who campaigned on an economy program, I am going to waste the taxpayer's money and call Boston long distance. It's ridiculous, it's insane—but I'm going to do it!"

His little blue eyes glittered and he moistened his lips with the tip of his tongue.

"Go ahead," he said hoarsely.

I replaced the telephone in its cradle.

"Nicky," I said, "this is probably the most remarkable coincidence in the history of criminal investigation: *a man was found murdered in his berth on last night's twelve-forty-seven from Washington!* He'd been dead about three hours, which would make it exactly right for Hadley."

"I thought it was something like that," said Nicky. "But you're wrong about its being a coincidence. It can't be. Where did you get that sentence?"

"It was just a sentence. It simply popped into my head."

"It couldn't have! It's not the sort of sentence that pops into one's head. If you had taught composition as long as I have, you'd know that when you ask someone for a sentence of ten words or so, you get an ordinary statement such as 'I like milk'—with the other words made up by a modifying clause like, 'because it is good for my health.' The sentence you offered related to a *particular situation.*"

"But I tell you I talked to no one this morning. And I was alone with you at the Blue Moon."

"You weren't with me all the time I paid my check," he said sharply. "Did you meet anyone while you were waiting on the sidewalk for me to come out of the Blue Moon?"

I shook my head. "I was outside for less than a minute before you joined me. You see, a couple of men came in while you were digging out your change and one of them bumped me, so I thought I'd wait—"

"Did you ever see them before?"

"Who?"

"The two men who came in," he said, the note of exasperation creeping into his voice again.

"Why, no—they weren't anyone I knew."

"Were they talking?"

"I guess so. Yes, they were. Quite absorbed in their conversation, as a matter of fact—otherwise, they would have noticed me and I would not have been bumped."

"Not many strangers come into the Blue Moon," he remarked.

"Do you think it was they?" I asked eagerly. "I think I'd know them again if I saw them."

Nicky's eyes narrowed. "It's possible. There had to be two—one to trail the victim in Washington and ascertain his berth number, the other to wait here and do the job. The Washington man would be likely to come down here afterwards. If there was theft as well as murder, it would be to divide the spoils. If it was just murder, he would probably have to come down to pay off his confederate."

I reached for the telephone.

"We've been gone less than half an hour," Nicky went on. "They were just coming in and service is slow at the Blue Moon. The one who walked all the way to Hadley must certainly be hungry and the other probably drove all night from Washington."

"Call me immediately if you make an arrest," I said into the phone and hung up.

Neither of us spoke a word while we waited. We paced the floor, avoiding each other almost as though we had done something we were ashamed of.

The telephone rang at last. I picked it up and listened. Then I said, "O.K." and turned to Nicky.

"One of them tried to escape through the kitchen but Winn had someone stationed at the back and they got him."

"That would seem to prove it," said Nicky with a frosty little smile.

I nodded agreement.

He glanced at his watch. "Gracious," he exclaimed, "I wanted to make an early start on my work this morning, and here I've already wasted all this time talking with you."

I let him get to the door. "Oh, Nicky," I called, "what was it you set out to prove?"

"That a chain of inferences could be logical and still not be true," he said.

"Oh."

"What are you laughing at?" he asked snappishly. And then he laughed too.

The Hands of Mr. Ottermole

Thomas Burke

*Thomas Burke didn't write many detective stories.
Around the last years of the nineteenth century, he
wrote "atmospheric" stories and novels of many kinds;
they've been unfairly neglected of late.*

*He did, however, write this crime story, and I can
not better the comment made on it by no less an expert
than Ellery Queen:*

"No finer crime story has ever been written, period."

At six o'clock of a January evening Mr. Whybrow was walking home through the cobweb alleys of London's East End. He had left the golden clamour of the great High Street to which the tram had brought him from the river and his daily work, and was now in the chessboard of byways that is called Mallon End. None of the rush and gleam of the High Street trickled into these byways. A few paces south—a flood tide of life, foaming and beating. Here—only slow-shuffling figures and muffled pulses. He was in the sink of London, the last refuge of European vagrants.

As though in tune with the street's spirit, he too walked slowly, with head down. It seemed that he was pondering some pressing trouble, but he was not. He had no trouble. He was walking slowly because he had been on his feet all day, and he was bent in abstraction because he was wondering whether the Missis would have herrings for his tea, or haddock; and he was trying to decide which would be the more tasty on a night like this. A wretched night it was, of damp and mist, and the mist wandered into his throat and his eyes, and the damp had settled on pavement and roadway, and where the sparse lamplight fell it sent up a greasy sparkle that chilled one to look at. By contrast it made his speculations more agreeable, and made him ready for that tea—whether herring or haddock. His eye turned from the glum bricks that made his horizon, and went forward half a mile. He saw a gas-lit kitchen, a flamy fire and a spread tea table. There was toast in the hearth and a singing kettle on the side and a piquant effusion of herrings, or maybe of haddock, or perhaps sausages. The vision gave his aching feet a throb of energy. He shook imperceptible damp from his shoulders, and hastened towards its reality.

But Mr. Whybrow wasn't going to get any tea that evening—or any other evening. Mr. Whybrow was going to die. Somewhere within a hundred yards of him another man was walking: a man much like Mr. Whybrow and much like any other man, but without the only quality that enables mankind to live peaceably together and not as madmen in a jungle. A man with a dead heart eating into itself and bringing forth the foul organisms that arise from death and corruption. And that thing in man's shape, on a whim or a settled idea—one cannot know—had said within himself that Mr. Whybrow should never taste another herring. Not that Mr. Whybrow had injured him. Not that he had any dislike of Mr. Whybrow. Indeed, he knew nothing of him save as a familiar figure about the streets. But, moved by a force that had taken possession of his empty cells, he had picked on Mr. Whybrow with that blind choice that makes us pick one restaurant table that has nothing to mark it from four or five other tables, or one apple from a dish of half a dozen equal apples; or that drives Nature to send a cyclone upon one corner of this planet, and destroy five hundred lives in that corner, and leave another five hundred in the same corner unharmed. So this man had picked on Mr. Whybrow, as he might have picked on you or me, had we been within his daily observation; and even now he was creeping through the blue-toned streets, nursing his large white hands, moving ever closer to Mr. Whybrow's tea table, and so closer to Mr. Whybrow himself.

He wasn't, this man, a bad man. Indeed, he had many of the social and amiable qualities, and passed as a respectable man, as most successful criminals do. But the thought had come into his mouldering mind that he would like to murder somebody, and, as he held no fear of God or man, he was going to do it, and would then go home to *his* tea. I don't say that flippantly, but as a statement of fact. Strange as it may seem to the humane, murderers must and do sit down to meals after a murder. There is no reason why they shouldn't, and many reasons why they should. For one thing, they need to keep their physical and mental vitality at full beat for the business of covering their crime. For another, the strain of their effort makes them hungry, and satisfaction at the accomplishment of a desired thing brings a feeling of relaxation towards human pleasures. It is accepted among non-murderers that the murderer is always overcome by fear for his safety and horror at his act; but this type is rare. His own safety is, of course, his immediate concern, but vanity is a marked quality of most murderers, and that, together with the thrill of conquest, makes him confident that he can secure it, and when he has restored his strength with food he goes about securing it as a young hostess goes about the arranging of her first big dinner—a little anxious, but no more. Criminologists and detectives tell us that *every* murderer, however intelligent or cunning, always makes one slip in his tactics—one little slip that brings the affair home to him. But that is only half true. It is true only of the murderers who are caught. Scores of murderers are not caught: therefore scores of murderers do not make any mistake at all. This man didn't.

As for horror or remorse, prison chaplains, doctors and lawyers have told us that of murderers they have interviewed under condemnation and the shadow of death, only one here and there has expressed any contrition for his act, or shown any sign of mental misery. Most of them display only exasperation at having been caught when so many have gone undiscovered, or indignation at being condemned for a perfectly reasonable act. However normal and humane they may have been before the murder, they are utterly without conscience after it. For what is conscience? Simply a polite nickname for superstition, which is a polite nickname for fear. Those who associate remorse with murder are, no doubt, basing their ideas on the world legend of the remorse of Cain, or are projecting their own frail minds into the mind of the murderer, and getting false reactions. Peaceable folk cannot hope to make contact with his mind, for they are not merely different in mental type from the murderer: they are different in their personal chemistry and construction. Some men can and do kill, not one man, but two or three, and go calmly about their daily affairs. Other men could not, under the most agonising provocation, bring themselves even to wound. It is men of this sort who imagine the murderer in torments of remorse and fear of the law, whereas he is actually sitting down to his tea.

The man with the large white hands was as ready for his tea as Mr. Whybrow was, but he had something to do before he went to it. When he had done that something, and made no mistake about it, he would be even more ready for it, and would go to it as comfortably as he went to it the day before, when his hands were stainless.

Walk on, then, Mr. Whybrow, walk on; and as you walk, look your last upon the familiar features of your nightly journey. Follow your jack-o'-lantern tea table. Look well upon its warmth and colour and kindness; feed your eyes with it, and tease your nose with its gentle domestic odours; for you will never sit down to it. Within ten minutes' pacing of you a pursuing phantom has spoken in his heart, and you are doomed. There you go—you and phantom—two nebulous dabs of mortality, moving through green air along pavements of powder blue, the one to kill, the other to be killed. Walk on. Don't annoy your burning feet by hurrying, for the more slowly you walk, the longer you will breathe the green air of this January dusk, and see the dreamy lamplight and the little shops, and hear the agreeable commerce of the London crowd and the haunting pathos of the street organ. These things are dear to you, Mr. Whybrow. You don't know it now, but in fifteen minutes you will have two seconds in which to realise how inexpressibly dear they are.

Walk on, then, across this crazy chessboard. You are in Lagos Street now, among the tents of the wanderers of Eastern Europe. A minute or so, and you are in Loyal Lane, among the lodging houses that shelter the useless and the beaten of London's camp followers. The lane holds the smell of them, and its soft darkness seems heavy with the wail of the futile. But you are not sensitive to impalpable things, and you plod through it, unseeing, as you do every evening, and come to Blean Street, and plod through that. From basement to sky rise the tenements of an alien colony. Their windows slot the ebony of their walls with lemon. Behind those windows strange life is moving, dressed with forms that are not of London or of England, yet, in essence, the same agreeable life that you have been living, and to-night will live no more. From high above you comes a voice crooning *The Song of Katta*. Through a window you see a family keeping a religious rite. Through another you see a woman pouring out tea for her husband. You see a man mending a pair of boots; a mother bathing her baby. You have seen all these things before, and never noticed them. You do not notice them now, but if you knew that you were never going to see them again, you would notice them. You never *will* see them again, not because your life has run its natural course, but because a man whom you have often passed in the street has at his own solitary pleasure decided to usurp the awful authority of nature, and destroy you. So perhaps it's as well that you don't notice them, for your part in them is ended. No more for you these pretty moments of our earthly travail: only one moment of terror, and then a plunging darkness.

Closer to you this shadow of massacre moves, and now he is twenty yards behind you. You can hear his footfall, but you do not turn your head. You are familiar with footfalls. You are in London, in the easy security of your daily territory, and footfalls behind you, your instinct tells you, are no more than a message of human company.

But can't you hear something in those footfalls—something that goes with a widdershins beat? Something that says: *Look out, look out. Beware, beware.* Can't you hear the very syllables of *mur-der-er, mur-der-er*? No; there is nothing in footfalls. They are neutral. The foot of villainy falls with the same quiet note as the foot of honesty. But those footfalls, Mr. Whybrow, are bearing on to you a pair of hands, and there *is* something in hands. Behind you that pair of hands is even now stretching its muscles in preparation for your end. Every minute of your days you have been seeing human hands. Have you ever realised the sheer horror of hands—those appendages that are a symbol for our moments of trust and affection and salutation? Have you thought of the sickening potentialities that lie within

41

the scope of that five-tentacled member? No, you never have; for all the human hands that you have seen have been stretched to you in kindness or fellowship. Yet, though the eyes can hate, and the lips can sting, it is only that dangling member that can gather the accumulated essence of evil, and electrify it into currents of destruction. Satan may enter into man by many doors, but in the hands alone can he find the servants of his will.

Another minute, Mr. Whybrow, and you will know all about the horror of human hands.

You are nearly home now. You have turned into your street—Caspar Street—and you are in the centre of the chessboard. You can see the front window of your little four-roomed house. The street is dark, and its three lamps give only a smut of light that is more confusing than darkness. It is dark—empty, too. Nobody about; no lights in the front parlours of the houses, for the families are at tea in their kitchens; and only a random glow in a few upper rooms occupied by lodgers. Nobody about but you and your following companion, and you don't notice him. You see him so often that he is never seen. Even if you turned your head and saw him, you would only say "Good-evening" to him, and walk on. A suggestion that he was a possible murderer would not even make you laugh. It would be too silly.

And now you are at your gate. And now you have found your door key. And now you are in, and hanging up your hat and coat. The Missis has just called a greeting from the kitchen, whose smell is an echo of that greeting (herrings!) and you have answered it, when the door shakes under a sharp knock.

Go away, Mr. Whybrow. Go away from that door. Don't touch it. Get right away from it. Get out of the house. Run with the Missis to the back garden, and over the fence.

Or call the neighbours. But don't touch that door. Don't, Mr. Whybrow, don't open . . .

Mr. Whybrow opened the door.

That was the beginning of what became known as London's Strangling Horrors. Horrors they were called because they were something more than murders: they were motiveless, and there was an air of black magic about them. Each murder was committed at a time when the street where the bodies were found was empty of any perceptible or possible murderer. There would be an empty alley. There would be a policeman at its end. He would turn his back on the empty alley for less than a minute. Then he would look round and run into the night with news of another strangling. And in any direction he looked nobody to be seen and no report to be had of anybody being seen. Or he would be on duty in a long-quiet street, and suddenly be called to a house of dead people whom a few seconds earlier he had seen alive. And, again, whichever way he looked nobody to be seen; and although police whistles put an immediate cordon around the area, and searched all houses, no possible murderer to be found.

The first news of the murder of Mr. and Mrs. Whybrow was brought by the station sergeant. He had been walking through Caspar Street on his way to the station for duty, when he noticed the open door of No. 98. Glancing in, he saw by the gaslight of the passage a motionless body on the floor. After a second look he blew his whistle, and when the constables answered him he took one to join him in a search of the house, and sent others to watch all neighbouring streets, and make inquiries at adjoining houses. But neither in the house nor in the streets was anything found to indicate the murderer. Neighbours on either side, and opposite, were questioned, but they had

43

seen nobody about, and had heard nothing. One had heard Mr. Whybrow come home—the scrape of his latchkey in the door was so regular an evening sound, he said, that you could set your watch by it for half past six—but he had heard nothing more than the sound of the opening door until the sergeant's whistle. Nobody had been seen to enter the house or leave it, by front or back, and the necks of the dead people carried no finger prints or other traces. A nephew was called in to go over the house, but he could find nothing missing; and anyway his uncle possessed nothing worth stealing. The little money in the house was untouched, and there were no signs of any disturbance of the property, or even of struggle. No signs of anything but brutal and wanton murder.

Mr. Whybrow was known to neighbours and workmates as a quiet, likeable, home-loving man; such a man as could not have any enemies. But, then, murdered men seldom have. A relentless enemy who hates a man to the point of wanting to hurt him seldom wants to murder him, since to do that puts him beyond suffering. So the police were left with an impossible situation: no clue to the murderer and no motive for the murders; only the fact that they had been done.

The first news of the affair sent a tremor through London generally, and an electric thrill through all Mallon End. Here was a murder of two inoffensive people, not for gain and not for revenge; and the murderer, to whom, apparently, killing was a casual impulse, was at large. He had left no traces, and, provided he had no companions, there seemed no reason why he should not remain at large. Any clear-headed man who stands alone, and has no fear of God or man, can, if he chooses, hold a city, even a nation, in subjection; but your everyday criminal is seldom clear-headed, and dislikes being lonely. He needs, if not the support of confederates, at least somebody to talk to; his vanity needs the satisfaction of perceiving at first hand the effect of his work. For this he will frequent bars and coffee shops and other public places. Then, sooner or later, in a glow of comradeship, he will utter the one word too much; and the nark, who is everywhere, has an easy job.

But though the doss houses and saloons and other places were "combed" and set with watches, and it was made known by whispers that good money and protection were assured to those with information, nothing attaching to the Whybrow case could be found. The murderer clearly had no friends and kept no company. Known men of this type were called up and questioned, but each was able to give a good account of himself; and in a few days the police were at a dead end. Against the constant public gibe that the thing had been done almost under their noses, they became restive, and for four days each man of the force was working his daily beat under a strain. On the fifth day they became still more restive.

It was the season of annual teas and entertainments for the children of the Sunday Schools, and on an evening of fog, when London was a world of groping phantoms, a small girl, in the bravery of best Sunday frock and shoes, shining face and new-washed hair, set out from Logan Passage for St. Michael's Parish Hall. She never got there. She was not actually dead until half past six, but she was as good as dead from the moment she left her mother's door. Somebody like a man, pacing the street from which the Passage led, saw her come out; and from the moment she was dead. Through the fog somebody's large white hands reached after her, and in fifteen minutes they were about her.

At half past six a whistle screamed trouble, and those answering it found the body of little Nellie Vrinoff in a warehouse entry in Minnow Street. The sergeant was first

45

among them, and he posted his men to useful points, ordering them here and there in the tart tones of repressed rage, and berating the officer whose beat the street was. "I saw you, Magson, at the end of the lane. What were you up to there? You were there ten minutes before you turned." Magson began an explanation about keeping an eye on a suspicious-looking character at that end, but the sergeant cut him short: "Suspicious characters be damned. You don't want to look for suspicious characters. You want to look for *murderers*. Messing about . . . and then this happens right where you ought to be. Now think what they'll say."

With the speed of ill news came the crowd, pale and perturbed; and on the story that the unknown monster had appeared again, and this time to a child, their faces streaked the fog with spots of hate and horror. But then came the ambulance and more police, and swiftly they broke up the crowd; and as it broke the sergeant's thought was thickened into words, and from all sides came low murmurs of "Right under their noses." Later inquiries showed that four people of the district, above suspicion, had passed that entry at intervals of seconds before the murder, and seen nothing and heard nothing. None of them had passed the child alive or seen her dead. None of them had seen anybody in the street except themselves. Again the police were left with no motive and with no clue.

And now the district, as you will remember, was given over, not to panic, for the London public never yields to that, but to apprehension and dismay. If these things were happening in their familiar streets, then anything might happen. Wherever people met—in the streets, the markets and the shops—they debated the one topic. Women took to bolting their windows and doors at the first fall of dusk. They kept their children closely under their eye. They did their shopping before dark, and watched anxiously, while pretending they weren't watching, for the return of their husbands from work. Under the Cockney's semi-humorous resignation to disaster, they did an hourly foreboding. By the whim of one man with a pair of hands the structure and tenor of their daily life were shaken, as they always can be shaken by any man contemptuous of humanity and fearless of its laws. They began to realise that the pillars that supported the peaceable society in which they lived were mere straws that anybody could snap; that laws were powerful only so long as they were obeyed; that the police were potent only so long as they were feared. By the power of his hands this one man had made a whole community do something new: he had made it think, and left it gasping at the obvious.

And then, while it was yet gasping under his first two strokes, he made his third. Conscious of the horror that his hands had created, and hungry as an actor who has once tasted the thrill of the multitude, he made fresh advertisement of his presence; and on Wednesday morning, three days after the murder of the child, the papers carried to the breakfast tables of England the story of a still more shocking outrage.

At 9.32 on Tuesday night a constable was on duty in Jarnigan Road, and at that time spoke to a fellow officer named Petersen at the top of Clemming Street. He had seen this officer walk down that street. He could swear that the street was empty at that time, except for a lame boot-black whom he knew by sight, and who passed him and entered a tenement on the side opposite that on which his fellow officer was walking. He had the habit, as all constables had just then, of looking constantly behind him and around him, whichever way he was walking, and he was certain that the street was empty. He passed his sergeant at 9.33, saluted him, and answered his inquiry for anything seen. He reported that he had seen nothing, and passed on. His beat ended at a short distance from Clemming Street, and, having paced it, he turned and came again at 9.34 to the top of the street. He had scarcely reached it before he heard the hoarse voice of the sergeant: "Gregory! You there? Quick. Here's another. My God, it's Petersen! Garotted. Quick, call 'em up!"

That was the third of the Strangling Horrors, of which there were to be a fourth and a fifth; and the five horrors were to pass into the unknown and unknowable. That is, unknown as far as authority and the public were concerned. The identity of the murderer *was* known, but to two men only. One was the murderer himself; the other was a young journalist.

This young man, who was covering the affairs for his paper, the *Daily Torch*, was no smarter than the other zealous newspaper men who were hanging about these byways in the hope of a sudden story. But he was patient, and he hung a little closer to the case than the other fellows, and by continually staring at it he at last raised the figure of the murderer like a genie from the stones on which he had stood to do his murders.

After the first few days the men had given up any attempt at exclusive stories, for there was none to be had. They met regularly at the police station, and what little information there was they shared. The officials were agreeable to them, but no more. The sergeant discussed with them the details of each murder; suggested possible explanations of the man's methods; recalled from the past those cases that had some similarity; and on the matter of motive reminded them of the motiveless Neill Cream and the wanton John Williams, and hinted that work was being done which would soon bring the business to an end; but about that work he would not say a word. The Inspector, too, was gracefully garrulous on the thesis of Murder, but whenever one of the party edged the talk towards what was being done in this immediate matter, he glided past it. Whatever the officials knew, they were not giving it to newspaper men. The business had fallen heavily upon them, and only by a capture made by their own efforts could they rehabilitate themselves in official and public esteem. Scotland Yard, of course, was at work, and had all the station's material; but the station's hope was that they themselves would have the honour of settling the affair; and however useful the coöperation of the Press might be in other cases, they did not want to risk a defeat by a premature disclosure of their theories and plans.

So the sergeant talked at large, and propounded one interesting theory after another, all of which the newspaper men had thought of themselves.

The young man soon gave up these morning lectures on the Philosophy of Crime, and took to wandering about the streets and making bright stories out of the effect of the murders on the normal life of the people. A melancholy job made more melancholy by the district. The littered roadways, the crestfallen houses, the bleared windows— all held the acid misery that evokes no sympathy: the misery of the frustrated poet. The misery was the creation of the aliens, who were living in this makeshift fashion because they had no settled homes, and would neither take the trouble to make a home where they *could* settle, nor get on with their wandering.

There was little to be picked up. All he saw and heard were indignant faces, and wild conjectures of the murderer's identity and of the secret of his trick of appearing and disappearing unseen. Since a policeman himself had fallen a victim, denunciations of the force had ceased, and the unknown was now invested with a cloak of legend. Men eyed other men, as though thinking: It might be *him*. It might be *him*. They were no longer looking for a man who had the air of a Madame Tussaud murderer; they were looking for a man, or perhaps some harridan woman, who had done these particular murders. Their thoughts ran mainly on the foreign set. Such ruffianism could scarcely belong to England, nor could the bewildering cleverness of the thing. So they turned to Roumanian gipsies and Turkish carpet sellers. There, clearly, would be found the "warm" spot. These Eastern fellows—they knew all sorts of tricks, and they had no real religion—nothing to hold them within bounds. Sailors returning from those parts had told tales of conjurors who made themselves invisible; and there were tales of Egyptian and Arab potions that were used for abysmally queer purposes. Perhaps it *was* possible to them; you never knew. They were so slick and cunning, and they had such gliding movements; no Englishman could melt away as they could. Almost certainly the murderer would be found to be one of that sort—with some dark trick of his own—and just because they were sure that he *was* a magician, they felt that it was useless to look for him. He was a power, able to hold them in subjection and to hold himself untouchable. Superstition, which so easily cracks the frail shell of reason, had got into them. He could do anything he chose: he would never be discovered. These two points they settled, and they went about the streets in a mood of resentful fatalism.

They talked of their ideas to the journalist in half tones, looking right and left, as though *HE* might overhear them and visit them. And though all the district was thinking of him and ready to pounce upon him, yet, so strongly had he worked upon them, that if any man in the street

—say, a small man of commonplace features and form—had cried "*I* am the Monster!" would their stifled fury have broken into flood and have borne him down and engulfed him? Or would they not suddenly have seen something unearthly in that everyday face and figure, something unearthly in his everyday boots, something unearthly about his hat, something that marked him as one whom none of their weapons could alarm or pierce? And would they not momentarily have fallen back from this devil, as the devil fell back from the Cross made by the sword of Faust, and so have given him time to escape? I do not know; but so fixed was their belief in his invincibility that it is at least likely that they would have made this hesitation, had such an occasion arisen. But it never did. To-day this commonplace fellow, his murder lust glutted, is still seen and observed among them as he was seen and observed all the time; but because nobody then dreamt, or now dreams, that he was what he was, they observed him then, and observe him now, as people observe a lamp-post.

Almost was their belief in his invincibility justified; for, five days after the murder of the policeman Petersen, when the experience and inspiration of the whole detective force of London were turned towards his identification and capture, he made his fourth and fifth strokes.

At nine o'clock that evening, the young newspaper man, who hung about every night until his paper was away, was strolling along Richards Lane. Richards Lane is a narrow street, partly a stall market, and partly residential. The young man was in the residential section, which carries on one side small working-class cottages, and on the other the wall of a railway goods yard. The great wall hung a blanket of shadow over the lane, and the shadow and the cadaverous outline of the now deserted market stalls gave it the appearance of a living lane that had been turned to frost in the moment between breath and death. The very lamps, that elsewhere were nimbuses of gold, had here the rigidity of gems. The journalist, feeling this message of frozen eternity, was telling himself that he was tired of the whole thing, when in one stroke the frost was broken. In the moment between one pace and another silence and darkness were racked by a high scream and through the scream a voice: "Help! help! *He's here!*"

Before he could think what movement to make, the lane came to life. As though its invisible populace had been waiting on that cry, the door of every cottage was flung open, and from them and from the alleys poured shadowy figures bent in question mark form. For a second or so they stood as rigid as the lamps; then a police whistle gave them direction, and the flock of shadows sloped up the street. The journalist followed them, and others followed him. From the main street and from surrounding streets they came, some risen from unfinished suppers, some disturbed in their ease of slippers and shirt sleeves, some stumbling on infirm limbs, and some upright, and armed with pokers or the tools of their trade. Here and there above the wavering cloud of heads moved the bold helmets of policemen. In one dim mass they surged upon a cottage whose doorway was marked by the sergeant and two constables; and voices of those behind urged them on with "Get in! Find him! Run round the back! Over the wall!" and those in front cried: "Keep back! Keep back!"

And now the fury of a mob held in thrall by unknown peril broke loose. He was here—on the spot. Surely this time he *could not* escape. All minds were bent upon the cottage; all energies thrust towards its doors and windows and roof; all thought was turned upon one unknown man and his extermination. So that no one man saw any other

52

man. No man saw the narrow, packed lane and the mass of struggling shadows, and all forgot to look among themselves for the monster who never lingered upon his victims. All forgot, indeed, that they, by their mass crusade of vengeance, were affording him the perfect hiding place. They saw only the house, and they heard only the rending of woodwork and the smash of glass at back and front, and the police giving orders or crying with the chase; and they pressed on.

But they found no murderer. All they found was news of murder and a glimpse of the ambulance, and for their fury there was no other object than the police themselves, who fought against this hampering of their work.

The journalist managed to struggle through to the cottage door, and to get the story from the constable stationed there. The cottage was the home of a pensioned sailor and his wife and daughter. They had been at supper, and at first it appeared that some noxious gas had smitten all three in mid-action. The daughter lay dead on the hearthrug, with a piece of bread and butter in her hand. The father had fallen sideways from his chair, leaving on his plate a filled spoon of rice pudding. The mother lay half under the table, her lap filled with the pieces of a broken cup and splashes of cocoa. But in three seconds the idea of gas was dismissed. One glance at their necks showed that this was the Strangler again; and the police stood and looked at the room and momentarily shared the fatalism of the public. They were helpless.

This was his fourth visit, making seven murders in all. He was to do, as you know, one more—and to do it that night; and then he was to pass into history as the unknown London horror, and return to the decent life that he had always led, remembering little of what he had done, and worried not at all by the memory. Why did he stop? Impossible to say. Why did he begin? Impossible again. It just happened like that; and if he thinks at all of those days and nights, I surmise that he thinks of them as we think of foolish or dirty little sins that we committed in childhood. We say that they were not really sins, because we were not then consciously ourselves: we had not come to realisation; and we look back at that foolish little creature that we once were, and forgive him because he didn't know. So, I think, with this man.

There are plenty like him. Eugene Aram, after the murder of Daniel Clarke, lived a quiet, contented life for fourteen years, unhaunted by his crime and unshaken in his self-esteem. Dr. Crippen murdered his wife, and then lived pleasantly with his mistress in the house under whose floor he had buried the wife. Constance Kent, found Not Guilty of the murder of her young brother, led a peaceful life for five years before she confessed. George Joseph Smith and William Palmer lived amiably among their fellows untroubled by fear or by remorse for their poisonings and drownings. Charles Peace, at the time he made his one unfortunate essay, had settled down into a respectable citizen with an interest in antiques. It happened that, after a lapse of time, these men were discovered, but more murderers than we guess are living decent lives to-day, and will die in decency, undiscovered and unsuspected. As this man will.

But he had a narrow escape, and it was perhaps this narrow escape that brought him to a stop. The escape was due to an error of judgment on the part of the journalist.

As soon as he had the full story of the affair, which took some time, he spent fifteen minutes on the telephone, sending the story through, and at the end of the fifteen minutes, when the stimulus of the business had left him, he felt physically tired and mentally dishevelled. He was not yet free to go home; the paper would not go away for another hour; so he turned into a bar for a drink and some sandwiches.

It was then, when he had dismissed the whole business from his mind, and was looking about the bar and admiring the landlord's taste in watch chains and his air of domination, and was thinking that the landlord of a well-conducted tavern had a more comfortable life than a newspaper man, that his mind received from nowhere a spark of light. He was not thinking about the Strangling Horrors; his mind was on his sandwich. As a public-house sandwich, it was a curiosity. The bread had been thinly cut, it was buttered, and the ham was not two months stale; it was ham as it should be. His mind turned to the inventor of this refreshment, the Earl of Sandwich, and then to George the Fourth, and then to the Georges, and to the legend of that George who was worried to know how the apple got into the apple dumpling. He wondered whether George would have been equally puzzled to know how the ham got into the ham sandwich, and how long it would have been before it occurred to him that the ham could not have got there unless somebody had put it there. He got up to order another sandwich, and in that moment a little active corner of his mind settled the affair. If there was ham in his sandwich, somebody must have put it there. If seven people had been murdered, somebody must have been there to murder them. There was no aeroplane or automobile that would go into a man's pocket; therefore that somebody must have escaped either by running away or standing still; and again therefore——

He was visualising the front-page story that his paper would carry if his theory were correct, and if—a matter of conjecture—his editor had the necessary nerve to make a bold stroke, when a cry of "Time, gentlemen, please! All out!" reminded him of the hour. He got up and went out into a world of mist, broken by the ragged discs of roadside puddles and the streaming lightning of motor buses. He was certain that he had *the* story, but, even if it were proved, he was doubtful whether the policy of his paper would permit him to print it. It had one great fault. It was truth, but it was impossible truth. It rocked the foundations of everything that newspaper readers believed and that newspaper editors helped them to believe. They might believe that Turkish carpet sellers had the gift of making themselves invisible. They would not believe this.

As it happened, they were not asked to, for the story was never written. As his paper had by now gone away, and as he was nourished by his refreshment and stimulated by his theory, he thought he might put in an extra half hour by testing that theory. So he began to look about for the man he had in mind—a man with white hair, and large white hands; otherwise an everyday figure whom nobody would look twice at. He wanted to spring his idea on this man without warning, and he was going to place himself within reach of a man armoured in legends of dreadfulness and grue. This might appear to be an act of supreme courage—that one man, with no hope of immediate outside support, should place himself at the mercy of one who was holding a whole parish in terror. But it wasn't. He didn't think about the risk. He didn't think about his duty to his employers or loyalty to his paper. He was moved simply by an instinct to follow a story to its end.

He walked slowly from the tavern and crossed into Fingal Street, making for Deever Market, where he had hope of finding his man. But his journey was shortened. At the corner of Lotus Street he saw him—or a man who looked like him. This street was poorly lit, and he could see little

56

of the man: but he *could* see white hands. For some twenty paces he stalked him; then drew level with him; and at a point where the arch of a railway crossed the street, he saw that this was his man. He approached him with the current conversational phrase of the district: "Well, seen anything of the murderer?" The man stopped to look sharply at him; then, satisfied that the journalist was not the murderer, said:

"Eh? No, nor's anybody else, curse it. Doubt if they ever will."

"I don't know. I've been thinking about them, and I've got an idea."

"So?"

"Yes. Came to me all of a sudden. Quarter of an hour ago. And I'd felt that we'd all been blind. It's been staring us in the face."

The man turned again to look at him, and the look and the movement held suspicion of this man who seemed to know so much. "Oh? Has it? Well, if you're so sure, why not give us the benefit of it?"

"I'm going to." They walked level, and were nearly at the end of the little street where it meets Deever Market, when the journalist turned casually to the man. He put a finger on his arm. "Yes, it seems to me quite simple now. But there's still one point I don't understand. One little thing I'd like to clear up. I mean the motive. Now, as man to man, tell me, Sergeant Ottermole, just *why* did you kill all those inoffensive people?"

The sergeant stopped, and the journalist stopped. There was just enough light from the sky, which held the reflected light of the continent of London, to give him a sight of the sergeant's face, and the sergeant's face was turned to him with a wide smile of such urbanity and charm that the journalist's eyes were frozen as they met it. The smile stayed for some seconds. Then said the sergeant: "Well, to tell you the truth, Mr. Newspaper Man, I don't know. I really don't know. In fact, I've been worried about it myself. But I've got an idea—just like you. Everybody knows that we can't control the workings of our minds. Don't they? Ideas come into our minds without asking. But everybody's supposed to be able to control his body. Why? Eh? We get our minds from lord-knows-where—from people who were dead hundreds of years before we were born. Mayn't we get out bodies in the same way? Our faces— our legs—our heads—they aren't completely ours. We don't make 'em. They come to us. And couldn't ideas come into our bodies like ideas come into our minds? Eh? Can't ideas live in nerve and muscle as well as in brain? Couldn't it be that parts of our bodies aren't really us, and couldn't ideas come into those parts all of a sudden, like ideas come into—into"—he shot his arms out, showing the great white-gloved hands and hairy wrists; shot them out so swiftly to the journalist's throat that his eyes never saw them—"into *my hands!*"

Try It My Way

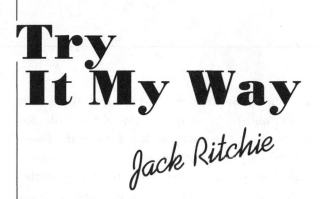

Jack Ritchie

Jack Ritchie may be the least well-known major writer
not only in the mystery genre but anywhere in
American literature.

His short stories have made many issues of mystery
magazines memorable. One of them, "A New Leaf,"
provided the basis for the Elaine May film.

He can do more in a few thousand words than most
writers can manage in a trilogy—and this story is an
exceptionally good example.

At four o'clock they thought of shutting off the water. I took the half-filled saucepan out of the sink and poured it into one of the big cookpots lined up on the floor.

Keegan stopped fooling with the automatic long enough to pour me a glass of vanilla extract from the quart bottle.

I took a couple of swallows and wiped my mouth on my sleeve. Then I pulled the bill of the guard cap lower and walked to the other end of the kitchen.

They were both in their underwear. Brock sat cross-legged, staring at the back of his big hands without interest, and Stevens hugged his legs tight to his chest, his eyes trying not to look up at me.

I grinned. "Here we got two types," I said. "Notice the nice gray hair, the clear healthy skin, and them baby-blue eyes on Stevens."

Turk was at the big window keeping an eye on the exercise yard. He turned his head. "A real nice grandpop. I remember the twinkle in his eye when he used his stick on my kidneys."

"Watch this, Turk," I said. I reached down and put my hand on Stevens' shoulder. He shrank away and began trembling.

Turk laughed. "That's good to see. I'm glad I lived so long."

"Stevens is remembering all the little things he used to

60

do to make life interesting for us," I said. "And now he's scared silly that we got better imaginations."

I shifted my smile to Brock. "Now, this here boy's got no imagination at all. He's got a free hand, but he can't think of the clever things like Stevens can."

Brock met my eyes. "I'm thinking of some now, Gomez."

I grinned at him a long time, and then I went to the window.

The guards were in a straggling arc around the three sides of the mess-hall wing. Some of them were standing, but most were taking it easy, hunkered on their heels and waiting for the warden to think of something.

I went back to my chair. "Keegan," I said, "I'll tell you about Davis. You're too young in here to remember him."

I lit a cigarette and exhaled smoke. "Davis was afraid of cats. Crazy afraid about them, and everybody knew it. And one day he made the mistake of using unrespectful words to Stevens, and he got tossed into the hole."

I put my feet on the table. "Davis had one peaceful day, and then he began screaming. Real interesting screaming, and it was all about how there was a cat in the hole with him."

Keegan took the clip out of the automatic and examined it.

"After a couple of hours Davis suddenly didn't make any more noise. When somebody bothered to wonder about that and take a look, he found Davis had beat his brains out against the wall."

I looked at Stevens. "In one of the corners was a black-as-spades cat licking his paws. Now, I wonder how he could of got in there."

Turk turned away from the window. "The warden's waving a hanky, and he's coming around to the main door."

Keegan got up and went into the dining hall, and I could hear his footsteps as he made his way through the emptiness of it. He began moving some of the tables and benches away from the double doors.

There would be guards in the corridor, but they wouldn't try to force their way in as long as we had Brock and Stevens with us.

In five minutes Keegan returned with Warden Cramer.

Cramer's eyes went to Brock and Stevens.

"They're doing just fine, Warden," I said. "But they might be a little chilly."

His eyes moved to the uniform I was wearing, and his mouth tightened. "This isn't going to get you anywhere, Gomez," he said.

"Tell us what we got to lose, Warden," I said. "I'm the short-timer here, and I got ninety years to wait."

He shifted his attention to Keegan. "For one thing, you got your lives to lose if anything happens to Brock or Stevens."

Keegan sipped his glass of extract and smiled at him.

"All right," Cramer snapped. "Let's have what you expect from me."

"A nice fast car and an open gate," Keegan said.

The warden's eyes were hard. "It wouldn't do you much good. You couldn't get far."

"We'll have Brock and Stevens along to show us the way," Keegan said. "Something clever should come to us when it gets dark."

Cramer walked over to Stevens and Brock. "They haven't tried anything rough on you, have they?"

"Just words," Brock said.

Cramer came back to us. "You have one hour to give this up."

I smiled. "And if we don't, Warden? Are you going to try what you haven't got nerve enough to do now?"

Cramer's face colored angrily.

"Remember," I said. "Keep it quiet and orderly out there. If you come for us, start thinking of words to use for Stevens' widow."

Keegan took the warden back out, and while he was gone I searched through the kitchen drawers until I found a whetstone. I began sharpening the nine-inch meat knife I carried.

When Keegan came back, he refilled our glasses.

Brock uncrossed his legs and rubbed circulation back into them. "Before that stuff goes to your head, Keegan, do some thinking. If Cramer lets you three get away with this, there won't be a guard safe in the country. He's not going to let that happen."

"Start hoping you're wrong," Turk said. "Work on it real hard."

I got to my feet and went over to Stevens. "Maybe I should cut off a few ears and toss them out into the yard for Cramer to admire. It might impress him that we mean business."

I got down on one knee in front of him. "Whose ears should it be, Stevens? Yours or Brock's?"

Stevens licked his lips and tried to look away, but his eyes came back to the knife in my hand.

I grabbed a handful of his hair and jerked his head back. I put the tip of my knife under his jaw. "You got two seconds to make up your mind."

His voice was the strangled whisper of terror. "Brock. Make it Brock."

I let go of him and stood up. "See, Brock," I said. "He wants his ears real bad. He don't love you at all when it comes to that."

Keegan was watching me. "Did you get your thrill, Gomez?"

"Sure," I said. "I got a mean streak in me, and it has to be fed."

Keegan lighted one of the cigars we'd found in Brock's uniform and took Turk's place at the window.

I went back to the table and sat down. "With Davis it was cats," I said. "With some people it's the dark or maybe high places."

I watched Turk pouring himself a drink. "I'm thinking of the time the drier in the laundry flared up," I said. "Just a short in the wiring and nothing to get excited about. Remember the size of Stevens' eyes when he thought he might get burned?"

I picked up a pack of book matches and lit one. I let it burn low, and Turk watched it. When I blew it out, Turk took the pack and went over to Stevens.

Turk stood there grinning, and then he tore one of the matches out of the pack and lit it.

Stevens' eyes got wide, and he backed away as he watched it burn.

"Let him alone, Turk," Keegan said from the window.

"All I want is a little fun," Turk said. "I got it coming."

Keegan came away from the window. "I just told you something, Turk."

Turk met his eyes for a few moments, and then he shrugged and walked away.

"Gomez, the idea man, and Turk, the pupil," Brock said. "You got nice company, Keegan."

"Stevens is with you," Keegan said. "Want to brag about him?"

Five o'clock passed and nothing happened. I relieved Keegan at the window and waved to the photographers who were behind the line of guards taking pictures.

The warden finished talking to a knot of reporters, and then he started through the guards.

"Cramer's coming back," I said. "And he hasn't got a car under his arm."

Keegan left to let him in. When he came back with the warden, they took seats at the table.

"Well?" Keegan asked.

"You might as well quit this before somebody gets hurt," Cramer said. "You're not getting out of here and that's that."

"We're stubborn and we think different," Keegan said. He glanced at the wrist watch he'd taken from Brock. "We're not going to drag this out until there's snow in hell. It's ten after five right now. We'll give you until seven."

"It's out of my hands," Cramer said. "I talked to the governor, and he says positively nothing doing."

"You got almost two hours to change his mind," I said.

"You know what will happen if you let anything happen to Brock or Stevens. You'll all be held equally responsible." Cramer's eyes went around the three of us and settled on Keegan. "You got sense enough to know that this won't work."

Keegan smiled thinly. "I'm the outdoor type, and I been in here six years. Don't count on me being able to think clear."

The warden got up. "Seven o'clock is going to come and go. It's not any special time on my clock."

He looked at the pots of water. "We can wait a long time out there. Longer than that will last."

When he was gone, Keegan sat at the table slowly smoking his cigar. It was quiet except for the sounds the guards made as they talked to each other in the yard.

At six Turk took my place at the window. I refilled my glass and lit a cigarette. "Cramer's got the notion that we don't have the guts to do like we say. I vote to build a fire under Stevens. He should get loud enough for even the governor to hear."

I let a whole book of matches flare up and tossed it at Stevens.

He shrieked as he skittered away from it. His face got pasty white and twitched with fright as he crouched in the corner watching me.

Keegan got up. "I thought I said words about doing things like that."

I glanced up. "Not to me."

"You're getting told now."

I looked at the bigness of his shoulders and the way his hands hung, ready to use.

I picked up the knife and smiled. "We'll leave it at your way for now. When it gets past seven we can argue about it."

At six thirty the dusk began pushing into the room. Keegan went to the light switch and tried it. Nothing happened.

It was a quarter to seven when the floodlights in the yard were turned on. Inside the kitchen pillars of light leaned against the windows.

Seven o'clock came and passed.

At ten after, I finished the last of the vanilla extract and threw the glass at the sink. "Now let's do it my way," I said. "Let them listen to Stevens die and they'll find us a car real fast."

Cellophane crackled as Keegan unwrapped another cigar. "Stop smacking your lips over Stevens and start thinking."

I sat on the edge of the table and began flipping the knife at the piece of light that lay over one corner of it and waited.

"Let's look at this thing with brains," Keegan said. "The party's over. We've had it."

I kept playing with the knife, and neither Turk nor I said anything.

Keegan went on. "Like Brock said, if we get away with it here, the same thing will be tried in every pen in the country. That's why Cramer's not going to let it happen."

"He'll have to," I said. "If we do it my way. We give them one body. That makes them know we got nothing more to lose. We can burn only once, and it'll be no cost to us to give them another corpse if they don't do like we say."

Keegan reached for his glass and then saw that it was empty. He pushed it away. "Use that beautiful imagination of yours now, Gomez. Suppose even that doesn't work. Start thinking about the hot seat."

Brock spoke from the darkness. "I watched a dozen of them take the walk. Ask me how scared they were."

I looked toward Brock and Stevens. They were in the shadows, but I knew they were watching and hoping.

Turk broke the silence. "It's not going to be a happy time for us when Brock and Stevens put on their uniforms again."

"I'm not looking forward to it either," Keegan said. "But it's better than frying."

There was another long quiet, and then Turk sighed. "That part about being alive persuades me."

Keegan's face came into the light as he leaned forward. "Make it unanimous, Gomez."

Brock spoke again. "It's something to see when they turn on the juice. They jump against the straps like the devil was burning inside of them. They're supposed to be dead in a second, but it don't look like that to me, Gomez. Not when they fight it like that."

I stuck the knife into the table. "I'm finished," I said. "Just like you are."

Keegan relaxed back into his chair. "First I finish this cigar. It'll be a long time before I taste another one."

And then I saw it.

I whirled toward the window, and it was there on the sill, a small silhouette against the light.

I whipped off my cap and smashed at it again and again until it was a broken stain on the stone.

"Jesus!" Turk said sharply. "You scared the hell out of me, jumping up like that. It wasn't nothing but a little cockroach."

Another floodlight flashed on outside, and a slant of light cut across the room and fell on Stevens.

Iciness gripped at my insides. Stevens knew about them now, and I knew what he was thinking about. He knew what I was afraid of. When we were back in our cells he'd know what to do to me.

I jerked the knife out of the table and went after him.

Keegan shouted and moved forward, but he was too late to stop me.

Keegan pulled at me, but I didn't let go of Stevens until I was through.

Keegan looked down at the body, and then his eyes met mine.

"All right, Gomez," he said quietly. "Now we got no choice. We try it your way."

The Two Bottles of Relish

Lord Dunsany

Edward John Moreton Drax Plunkett—usually known by his title as the eighteenth Baron, Lord Dunsany— wrote plays, stories, poems, and a veritable cascade of wonderful material of all sorts. He was better known some years ago than he has been lately, but I don't doubt that a revival is on the way.

This story scarcely needs revival—once you've read it you are most unlikely to forget it. It's been called the single best murder story ever written, and though I think I might dispute that, there would be no keeping it out of the top dozen.

Smithers is my name. I'm what you might call a small
man and in a small way of business. I travel for
Num-numo, a relish for meats and savouries—the world-
famous relish I ought to say. It's really quite good, no
deleterious acids in it, and does not affect the heart; so it
is quite easy to push. I wouldn't have got the job if it
weren't. But I hope some day to get something that's harder
to push, as of course the harder they are to push, the better
the pay. At present I can just make my way, with nothing
at all over; but then I live in a very expensive flat. It
happened like this, and that brings me to my story. And
it isn't the story you'd expect from a small man like me,
yet there's nobody else to tell it. Those that know anything
of it besides me are all for hushing it up. Well, I was
looking for a room to live in in London when first I got my
job. It had to be in London, to be central; and I went to
a block of buildings, very gloomy they looked, and saw
the man that ran them and asked him for what I wanted.
Flats they called them; just a bedroom and a sort of a
cupboard. Well, he was showing a man round at the time
who was a gent, in fact more than that, so he didn't take
much notice of me—the man that ran all those flats didn't,
I mean. So I just ran behind for a bit, seeing all sorts of
rooms and waiting till I could be shown my class of thing.
We came to a very nice flat, a sitting room, bedroom and
bathroom, and a sort of little place that they called a hall.

And that's how I came to know Linley. He was the bloke that was being shown round.

"Bit expensive," he said.

And the man that ran the flats turned away to the window and picked his teeth. It's funny how much you can show by a simple thing like that. What he meant to say was that he'd hundreds of flats like that, and thousands of people looking for them, and he didn't care who had them or whether they all went on looking. There was no mistaking him, somehow. And yet he never said a word, only looked away out of the window and picked his teeth. And I ventured to speak to Mr. Linley then; and I said, "How about it, sir, if I paid half, and shared it? I wouldn't be in the way, and I'm out all day, and whatever you said would go, and really I wouldn't be no more in your way than a cat."

You may be surprised at my doing it; and you'll be much more surprised at him accepting it—at least, you would if you knew me, just a small man in a small way of business. And yet I could see at once that he was taking to me more than he was taking to the man at the window.

"But there's only one bedroom," he said.

"I could make up my bed easy in that little room there," I said.

"The Hall," said the man, looking round from the window, without taking his toothpick out.

"And I'd have the bed out of the way and hid in the cupboard by any hour you like," I said.

He looked thoughtful, and the other man looked out over London; and in the end, do you know, he accepted.

"Friend of yours?" said the flat man.

"Yes," answered Mr. Linley.

It was really very nice of him.

I'll tell you why I did it. Able to afford it? Of course not. But I heard him tell the flat man that he had just come

71

down from Oxford and wanted to live for a few months in London. It turned out he wanted just to be comfortable and do nothing for a bit while he looked things over and chose a job, or probably just as long as he could afford it. Well, I said to myself, what's the Oxford manner worth in business, especially a business like mine? Why, simply everything you've got. If I picked up only a quarter of it from this Mr. Linley I'd be able to double my sales, and that would soon mean I'd be given something a lot harder to push, with perhaps treble the pay. Worth it every time. And you can make a quarter of an education go twice as far again, if you're careful with it. I mean you don't have to quote the whole of the *Inferno* to show that you've read Milton; half a line may do it.

Well, about that story I have to tell. And you mightn't think that a little man like me could make you shudder. Well, I soon forgot about the Oxford manner when we settled down in our flat. I forgot it in the sheer wonder of the man himself. He had a mind like an acrobat's body, like a bird's body. It didn't want education. You didn't notice whether he was educated or not. Ideas were always leaping up in him, things you'd never have thought of. And not only that, but if any ideas were about, he'd sort of catch them. Time and again I've found him knowing just what I was going to say. Not thought reading, but what they call intuition. I used to try to learn a bit about chess, just to take my thoughts off Num-numo in the evening, when I'd done with it. But problems I never could do. Yet he'd come along and glance at my problem and say, "You probably move that piece first," and I'd say, "But where?" and he'd say, "Oh, one of those three squares." And I'd say, "But it will be taken on all of them." And the piece a queen all the time, mind you. And he'd say, "Yes, it's doing no good there: you're probably meant to lose it."

And, do you know, he'd be right.

You see, he'd been following out what the other man had been thinking. That's what he'd been doing.

Well, one day there was that ghastly murder at Unge. I don't know if you remember it. But Steeger had gone down to live with a girl in a bungalow on the North Downs, and that was the first we had heard of him.

The girl had £200, and he got every penny of it, and she utterly disappeared. And Scotland Yard couldn't find her.

Well, I'd happened to read that Steeger had bought two bottles of Num-numo; for the Otherthorpe police had found out everything about him, except what he did with the girl; and that of course attracted my attention, or I should have never thought again about the case or said a word of it to Linley. Num-numo was always on my mind, as I always spent every day pushing it, and that kept me from forgetting the other thing. And so one day I said to Linley, "I wonder with all that knack you have for seeing through a chess problem, and thinking of one thing and another, that you don't have a go at that Otherthorpe mystery. It's a problem as much as chess," I said.

"There's not the mystery in ten murders that there is in one game of chess," he answered.

"It's beaten Scotland Yard," I said.

"Has it?" he asked.

"Knocked them endwise," I said.

"It shouldn't have done that," he said. And almost immediately after he said, "What are the facts?"

We were both sitting at supper, and I told him the facts, as I had them straight from the papers. She was a pretty blonde, she was small, she was called Nancy Elth, she had £200, they lived at the bungalow for five days. After that he stayed there for another fortnight, but nobody ever saw her alive again. Steeger said she had gone to South America, but later said he had never said South America, but South Africa. None of her money remained in the bank where she had kept it, and Steeger was shown to have come by at least £150 just at that time. Then Steeger turned out to be a vegetarian, getting all his food from the greengrocer, and that made the constable in the village of Unge suspicious of him, for a vegetarian was something new to the constable. He watched Steeger after that, and it's well he did, for there was nothing that Scotland Yard asked him that he couldn't tell them about him, except of course the one thing. And he told the police at Otherthorpe five or six miles away, and they came and took a hand at it too. They were able to say for one thing that he never went outside the bungalow and its tidy garden ever since she disappeared. You see, the more they watched him the more suspicious they got, as you naturally do if you're watching a man; so that very soon they were watching every move he made, but if it hadn't been for his being a vegetarian they'd never have started to suspect him, and there wouldn't have been enough evidence even for Linley. Not that they found out anything much against him, except that £150 dropping in from nowhere, and it was Scotland Yard that found that, not the police of Otherthorpe. No, what the constable of Unge found out was about the larch trees, and that beat Scotland Yard utterly, and beat Linley up to the very last, and of course it beat me. There were ten larch trees in the bit of a garden, and he'd made some sort of an arrangement with the landlord, Steeger had, before he took the bungalow, by which he could do what he liked with the larch trees. And then from about the time that little Nancy Elth must have died he cut every one of them down. Three times a day he went at it for nearly a week, and when they were all down he cut them all up into logs

74

no more than two foot long and laid them all in neat heaps. You never saw such work. And what for? To give an excuse for the axe was one theory. But the excuse was bigger than the axe; it took him a fortnight, hard work every day. And he could have killed a little thing like Nancy Elth without an axe, and cut her up too. Another theory was that he wanted firewood, to make away with the body. But he never used it. He left it all standing there in those neat stacks. It fairly beat everybody.

Well, those are the facts I told Linley. Oh yes, and he bought a big butcher's knife. Funny thing, they all do. And yet it isn't so funny after all; if you've got to cut a woman up, you've got to cut her up; and you can't do that without a knife. Then, there were some negative facts. He hadn't burned her. Only had a fire in the small stove now and then, and only used it for cooking. They got on to that pretty smartly, the Unge constable did, and the men that were lending him a hand from Otherthorpe. There were some little woody places lying round, shaws they call them in that part of the country, the country people do, and they could climb a tree handy and unobserved and get a sniff at the smoke in almost any direction it might be blowing. They did that now and then, and there was no smell of flesh burning, just ordinary cooking. Pretty smart of the Otherthorpe police that was, though of course it didn't help to hang Steeger. Then later on the Scotland Yard men went down and got another fact—negative, but narrowing things down all the while. And that was that the chalk under the bungalow and under the little garden had none of it been disturbed. And he'd never been outside it since Nancy disappeared. Oh yes, and he had a big file besides the knife. But there was no sign of any ground bones found on the file, or any blood on the knife. He'd washed them of course. I told all that to Linley.

Now I ought to warn you before I go any further. I am a small man myself and you probably don't expect anything horrible from me. But I ought to warn you this man was a murderer, or at any rate somebody was; the woman had been made away with, a nice pretty little girl too, and the man that had done that wasn't necessarily going to stop at things you might think he'd stop at. With the mind to do a thing like that, and with the long thin shadow of the rope to drive him further, you can't say what he'll stop at. Murder tales seem nice things sometimes for a lady to sit and read all by herself by the fire. But murder isn't a nice thing, and when a murderer's desperate and trying to hide his tracks he isn't even as nice as he was before. I'll ask you to bear that in mind. Well, I've warned you.

So I says to Linley, "And what do you make of it?"

"Drains?" said Linley.

"No," I says, "you're wrong there. Scotland Yard has been into that. And the Otherthorpe people before them. They've had a look in the drains, such as they are, a little thing running into a cesspool beyond the garden; and nothing has gone down it—nothing that oughtn't to have, I mean."

He made one or two other suggestions, but Scotland Yard had been before him in every case. That's really the crab of my story, if you'll excuse the expression. You want a man who sets out to be a detective to take his magnifying glass and go down to the spot; to go to the spot before everything; and then to measure the footmarks and pick up the clues and find the knife that the police have overlooked. But Linley never even went near the place, and he hadn't got a magnifying glass, not as I ever saw, and Scotland Yard were before him every time.

In fact they had more clues than anybody could make head or tail of. Every kind of clue to show that he'd murdered the poor little girl; every kind of clue to show that he hadn't disposed of the body; and yet the body wasn't there. It wasn't in South America either, and not much more likely in South Africa. And all the time, mind you, that enormous bunch of chopped larchwood, a clue that was staring everyone in the face and leading nowhere. No, we didn't seem to want any more clues, and Linley never went near the place. The trouble was to deal with the clues we'd got. I was completely mystified; so was Scotland Yard; and Linley seemed to be getting no forwarder; and all the while the mystery was hanging on me. I mean if it were not for the trifle I'd chanced to remember, and if it were not for one chance word I said to Linley, that mystery would have gone the way of all the other mysteries that men have made nothing of, a darkness, a little patch of night in history.

Well, the fact was Linley didn't take much interest in it at first, but I was so absolutely sure that he could do it that I kept him to the idea. "You can do chess problems," I said.

"That's ten times harder," he said, sticking to his point.

"Then why don't you do this?" I said.

"Then go and take a look at the board for me," said Linley.

That was his way of talking. We'd been a fortnight together, and I knew it by now. He meant me to go down to the bungalow at Unge. I know you'll say why didn't he go himself; but the plain truth of it is that if he'd been tearing about the countryside he'd never have been thinking, whereas sitting there in his chair by the fire in our flat there was no limit to the ground he could cover, if you follow my meaning. So down I went by train next day, and got out at Unge station. And there were the North Downs rising up before me, somehow like music.

"It's up there, isn't it?" I said to the porter.

"That's right," he said. "Up there by the lane; and mind to turn to your right when you get to the old yew tree, a very big tree, you can't mistake it, and then . . ." and he told me the way so that I couldn't go wrong. I found them all like that, very nice and helpful. You see, it was Unge's day at last. Everyone had heard of Unge now; you could have got a letter there any time just then without putting the county or post town; and this was what Unge had to show. I dare say if you tried to find Unge now . . . well, anyway, they were making hay while the sun shone.

Well, there the hill was, going up into sunlight, going up like a song. You don't want to hear about the spring, and all the May rioting, and the colour that came down over everything later on in the day, and all those birds; but I thought, "What a nice place to bring a girl to." And then when I thought that he'd killed her there, well I'm only a small man, as I said, but when I thought of her on that hill with all the birds singing, I said to myself, "Wouldn't it be odd if it turned out to be me after all that got that man killed, if he did murder her." So I soon found my way up to the bungalow and began prying about, looking over the hedge into the garden. And I didn't find much, and I found nothing at all that the police hadn't found already, but there were those heaps of larch logs staring me in the face and looking very queer.

I did a lot of thinking, leaning against the hedge, breathing the smell of the may, and looking over the top of it at the larch logs, and the neat little bungalow the other side of the garden. Lots of theories I thought of, till I came to the best thought of all; and that was that if I left the thinking to Linley, with his Oxford-and-Cambridge education, and only brought him the facts, as he had told me, I should be doing more good in my way than if I tried to do any big thinking. I forgot to tell you that I had gone to Scotland Yard in the morning. Well, there wasn't really much to tell. What they asked me was what I wanted. And, not having an answer exactly ready, I didn't find out very much from them. But it was quite different at Unge; everyone was most obliging; it was their day there, as I said. The constable let me go indoors, so long as I didn't touch anything, and he gave me a look at the garden from the inside. And I saw the stumps of the ten larch trees, and I noticed one thing that Linley said was very observant of me, not that it turned out to be any use, but anyway I was doing my best: I noticed that the stumps had been all chopped anyhow. And from that I thought that the man that did it didn't know much about chopping. The constable said that was a deduction. So then I said that the axe was blunt when he used it; and that certainly made the constable think, though he didn't actually say I was right this time. Did I tell you that Steeger never went outdoors, except to the little garden to chop wood, ever since Nancy disappeared? I think I did. Well, it was perfectly true. They'd watched him night and day, one or another of them, and the Unge constable told me that himself. That limited things a good deal. The only thing I didn't like about it was that I felt Linley ought to have found all that out instead of ordinary policemen, and I felt that he could have too. There'd have been romance in a story like that. And they'd never have done it if the news hadn't gone round that the man was a vegetarian and only dealt at the greengrocer's. Likely as not even that was only started out of pique by the butcher. It's queer what little things may trip a man up. Best to keep straight is my motto. But perhaps I'm straying a bit away from my story. I should like to do that for ever—forget that it ever was; but I can't.

Well, I picked up all sorts of information; clues I suppose

I should call it in a story like this, though they none of them seemed to lead anywhere. For instance, I found out everything he ever bought at the village, I could even tell you the kind of salt he bought, quite plain with no phosphates in it, that they sometimes put in to make it tidy. And then he got ice from the fishmonger's, and plenty of vegetables, as I said, from the greengrocer, Mergin & Sons. And I had a bit of a talk over it all with the constable. Slugger he said his name was. I wondered why he hadn't come in and searched the place as soon as the girl was missing. "Well, you can't do that," he said. "And besides, we didn't suspect at once, not about the girl, that is. We only suspected there was something wrong about him on account of him being a vegetarian. He stayed a good fortnight after the last that was seen of her. And then we slipped in like a knife. But, you see, no one had been enquiring about her, there was no warrant out."

"And what did you find?" I asked Slugger, "when you went in?"

"Just a big file," he said, "and the knife and the axe that he must have got to chop her up with."

"But he got the axe to chop trees with," I said.

"Well, yes," he said, but rather grudgingly.

"And what did he chop them for?" I asked.

"Well, of course, my superiors has theories about that," he said, "that they mightn't tell to everybody."

You see, it was those logs that were beating them.

"But did he cut her up at all?" I asked.

"Well, he said that she was going to South America," he answered. Which was really very fair-minded of him.

I don't remember now much else that he told me. Steeger left the plates and dishes all washed up and very neat, he said.

Well, I brought all this back to Linley, going up by the

80

train that started just about sunset. I'd like to tell you about the late spring evening, so calm over that grim bungalow, closing in with a glory all round it as though it were blessing it; but you'll want to hear of the murder. Well, I told Linley everything, though much of it didn't seem to me to be worth the telling. The trouble was that the moment I began to leave anything out, he'd know it, and make me drag it in. "You can't tell what may be vital," he'd say. "A tin tack swept away by a housemaid might hang a man."

All very well, but be consistent, even if you are educated at Eton and Harrow, and whenever I mentioned Num-numo, which after all was the beginning of the whole story, because he wouldn't have heard of it if it hadn't been for me, and my noticing that Steeger had bought two bottles of it, why then he said that things like that were trivial and we should keep to the main issues. I naturally talked a bit about Num-numo, because only that day I had pushed close on fifty bottles of it in Unge. A murder certainly stimulates people's minds, and Steeger's two bottles gave me an opportunity that only a fool could have failed to make something of. But of course all that was nothing at all to Linley.

You can't see a man's thoughts, and you can't look into his mind, so that all the most exciting things in the world can never be told of. But what I think happened all that evening with Linley, while I talked to him before supper, and all through supper, and sitting smoking afterwards in front of our fire, was that his thoughts were stuck at a barrier there was no getting over. And the barrier wasn't the difficulty of finding ways and means by which Steeger might have made away with the body, but the impossibility of finding why he chopped those masses of wood every day for a fortnight, and paid, as I'd just found out, £25 to his landlord to be allowed to do it. That's what was beating

81

Linley. As for the ways by which Steeger might have hidden
the body, it seemed to me that every way was blocked by
the police. If you said he buried it, they said the chalk
was undisturbed; if you said he carried it away, they said
he never left the place; if you said he burned it, they said
no smell of burning was ever noticed when the smoke blew
low, and when it didn't they climbed trees after it. I'd taken
to Linley wonderfully, and I didn't have to be educated to
see there was something big in a mind like his, and I
thought that he could have done it. When I saw the police
getting in before him like that, and no way that I could
see of getting past them, I felt real sorry.

Did anyone come to the house, he asked me once or
twice. Did anyone take anything away from it? But we
couldn't account for it that way. Then perhaps I made some
suggestion that was no good, or perhaps I started talking
of Num-numo again, and he interrupted me rather sharply.

"But what would you do, Smithers?" he said. "What
would you do yourself?"

"If I'd murdered poor Nancy Elth?" I asked.

"Yes," he said.

"I can't ever imagine doing such a thing," I told him.

He sighed at that, as though it were something against
me.

"I suppose I should never be a detective," I said. And
he just shook his head.

Then he looked broodingly into the fire for what seemed
an hour. And then he shook his head again. We both went
to bed after that.

I shall remember the next day all my life. I was till
evening, as usual, pushing Num-numo. And we sat down
to supper about nine. You couldn't get things cooked at
those flats, so of course we had it cold. And Linley began
with a salad. I can see it now, every bit of it. Well, I was

still a bit full of what I'd done in Unge, pushing Num-numo. Only a fool, I know, would have been unable to push it there; but still, I *had* pushed it; and about fifty bottles, forty-eight to be exact, are something in a small village, whatever the circumstances. So I was talking about it a bit; and then all of a sudden I realized that Num-numo was nothing to Linley, and I pulled myself up with a jerk. It was really very kind of him; do you know what he did? He must have known at once why I stopped talking, and he just stretched out a hand and said, "Would you give me a little of your Num-numo for my salad?"

I was so touched I nearly gave it him. But of course you don't take Num-numo with salad. Only for meats and savouries. That's on the bottle.

So I just said to him, "Only for meats and savouries." Though I don't know what savouries are. Never had any.

I never saw a man's face go like that before.

He seemed still for a whole minute. And nothing speaking about him but that expression. Like a man that's seen a ghost, one is tempted to write. But it wasn't really at all. I'll tell you what he looked like. Like a man that's seen something that no one has ever looked at before, something he thought couldn't be.

And then he said in a voice that was all quite changed, more low and gentle and quiet it seemed, "No good for vegetables, eh?"

"Not a bit," I said.

And at that he gave a kind of sob in his throat. I hadn't thought he could feel things like that. Of course I didn't know what it was all about; but, whatever it was, I thought all that sort of thing would have been knocked out of him at Eton and Harrow, an educated man like that. There were no tears in his eyes, but he was feeling something horribly.

And then he began to speak with big spaces between his words, saying, "A man might make a mistake perhaps, and use Num-numo with vegetables."

"Not twice," I said. What else could I say?

And he repeated that after me as though I had told of the end of the world, and adding an awful emphasis to my words, till they seemed all clammy with some frightful significance, and shaking his head as he said it.

Then he was quite silent.

"What is it?" I asked.

"Smithers," he said.

"Yes," I said.

"Smithers," said he.

And I said, "Well?"

"Look here, Smithers," he said, "you must phone down to the grocer at Unge and find out from him this."

"Yes?" I said.

"Whether Steeger bought those two bottles, as I expect he did, on the same day, and not a few days apart. He couldn't have done that."

I waited to see if any more was coming, and then I ran out and did what I was told. It took me some time, being after nine o'clock, and only then with the help of the police. About six days apart they said; and so I came back and told Linley. He looked up at me so hopefully when I came in, but I saw that it was the wrong answer by his eyes.

You can't take things to heart like that without being ill, and when he didn't speak I said, "What you want is a good brandy, and go to bed early."

And he said, "No. I must see someone from Scotland Yard. Phone round to them. Say here at once."

But I said, "I can't get an inspector from Scotland Yard to call on us at this hour."

His eyes were all lit up. He was all there all right.

84

"Then tell them," he said, "they'll never find Nancy Elth. Tell one of them to come here, and I'll tell him why." And he added, I think only for me, "They must watch Steeger, till one day they get him over something else."

And, do you know, he came. Inspector Ulton; he came himself.

While we were waiting I tried to talk to Linley. Partly curiosity, I admit. But I didn't want to leave him to those thoughts of his, brooding away by the fire. I tried to ask him what it was all about. But he wouldn't tell me. "Murder is horrible," is all he would say. "And as a man covers his tracks up it only gets worse."

He wouldn't tell me. "There are tales," he said, "that one never wants to hear."

That's true enough. I wish I'd never heard this one. I never did actually. But I guessed it from Linley's last words to Inspector Ulton, the only ones that I overheard. And perhaps this is the point at which to stop reading my story, so that you don't guess it too; even if you think you want murder stories. For don't you rather want a murder story with a bit of a romantic twist, and not a story about real foul murder? Well, just as you like.

In came Inspector Ulton, and Linley shook hands in silence, and pointed the way to his bedroom; and they went in there and talked in low voices, and I never heard a word.

A fairly hearty-looking man was the inspector when they went into that room.

They walked through our sitting room in silence when they came out, and together they went into the hall, and there I heard the only words they said to each other. It was the inspector that first broke that silence.

"But why," he said, "did he cut down the trees?"

"Solely," said Linley, "in order to get an appetite."

The Rubber Trumpet

Roy Vickers

*The Department of Dead Ends isn't well enough
known, though people from Ellery Queen to yours truly
have been admiring it for years. I have to tell you that
the story to follow—the first Department of Dead Ends
story—is fiction and not fact.*

When Ellery Queen's Mystery Magazine *first
published it, an editor's note said that nobody was
quite sure whether it was fact or fiction. That is high
praise for any story. Higher praise might be that, in
the nearly fifty years since its first appearance, nobody
has come close to the total control and command Roy
Vickers displays here.*

*There are lots of other Department of Dead Ends
stories. As far as I know, no two published collections
contain exactly the same stories. I don't know what the
reason for that is, but I suspect Detective-Inspector
Rason could find one. . . .*

I f you were to enquire at Scotland Yard for the De-partment of Dead Ends you might be told, in all sincerity, that there was no such thing, because it is not called by that name nowadays. All the same, if it has no longer a room to itself, you may rest assured that its spirit hovers over the index files of which we are all so justly proud.

The Department came into existence in the spacious days of King Edward VII, and it took everything that the other departments rejected. For instance, it noted and filed all those clues that had the exasperating effect of proving a palpably guilty man innocent. Its shelves were crowded with exhibits that might have been in the Black Museum —but were not. Its photographs were a perpetual irritation to all rising young detectives, who felt that they ought to have found the means of putting them in the Rogues' Gallery.

To the Department, too, were taken all those members of the public who insist on helping the police with obviously irrelevant information and preposterous theories. The one passport to the Department was a written statement by the senior officer in charge of the case that the information offered was absurd.

Judged by the standards of reason and common sense, its files were mines of misinformation. It proceeded largely by guesswork. On one occasion it hanged a murderer by accidentally punning on his name.

It was the function of the Department to connect persons and things that had no logical connection. In short, it stood for the antithesis of scientific detection. It played always for a lucky fluke—to offset the lucky fluke by which the criminal so often eludes the police. Often it muddled one crime with another and arrived at the correct answer by wrong reasoning.

As in the case of George Muncey and the rubber trumpet.

And note, please, that the rubber trumpet had nothing logically to do with George Muncey, nor the woman he murdered, nor the circumstances in which he murdered her.

Until the age of twenty-six George Muncey lived with his widowed mother in Chichester, the family income being derived from a chemist's shop, efficiently controlled by Mrs. Muncey with the aid of a manager and two assistants, of whom latterly George was one. Of his early youth we know only that he won a scholarship at a day-school, tenable for three years, which was cancelled at the end of a year though not, apparently, for misconduct. He failed several times to obtain his pharmaceutical certificate, with the result that he was eventually put in charge of the fancy soaps, the hot water bottles and the photographic accessories.

For this work he received two pounds per week. Every Saturday he handed the whole of it to his mother, who returned him fifteen shillings for pocket money. She had no need of the balance and only took it in order to nourish his self-respect. He did not notice that she bought his clothes and met all his other expenses.

George had no friends and very little of what an ordinary young man would regard as pleasure. He spent nearly all his spare time with his mother, to whom he was devoted. She was an amiable but very domineering woman and she does not seem to have noticed that her son's affection had in it a quality of childishness—that he liked her to form his opinions for him and curtail his liberties.

After his mother's death he did not resume his duties at the shop. For some eight months he mooned about Chichester. Then, the business having been sold and probate granted, he found himself in possession of some eight hundred pounds, with another two thousand pounds due to him in three months. He does not seem to have understood this part of the transaction—for he made no application for the two thousand, and as the solicitors could not find him until his name came into the papers, the two thousand remained intact for his defense.

That he was a normal but rather backward young man is proved by the fact that the walls of his bedroom were liberally decorated with photographs of the actresses of the moment and pictures of anonymous beauties cut from the more sporting weeklies. Somewhat naïvely he bestowed this picture gallery as a parting gift on the elderly cook.

He drew the whole of the eight hundred pounds in notes and gold, said goodbye to his home and went up to London. He stumbled on cheap and respectable lodgings in Pimlico. Then, in a gauche, small-town way, he set out to see life.

It was the year when *The Merry Widow* was setting all London a-whistling. Probably on some chance recommendation, he drifted to Daly's Theatre, where he bought himself a seat in the dress-circle.

It was the beginning of the London season and we may assume that he would have felt extremely self-conscious sitting in the circle in his ready-made lounge suit, had there not happened to be a woman also in morning-dress next to him.

The woman was a Miss Hilda Callermere. She was forty-three and if she escaped positive ugliness she was certainly without any kind of physical attractiveness, though she was neat in her person and reasonably well-dressed, in an old-fashioned way.

Eventually to the Department of Dead Ends came the whole story of his strange courtship.

There is a curious quality in the manner in which these two slightly unusual human beings approached one another. They did not speak until after the show, when they were wedged together in the corridor. Their voices seem to come to us out of a fog of social shyness and vulgar gentility. And it was she who took the initiative.

"If you'll excuse me speaking to you without an introduction, we seem to be rather out of it, you and I, what with one thing and another."

His reply strikes us now as somewhat unusual.

"Yes, rather!" he said. "Are you coming here again?"

"Yes, rather! I sometimes come twice a week."

During the next fortnight they both went three times to *The Merry Widow*, but on the first two of these occasions they missed each other. On the third occasion, which was a Saturday night, Miss Callermere invited George Muncey to walk with her on the following morning in Battersea Park.

Here shyness dropped from them. They slipped quite suddenly on to an easy footing of friendship. George Muncey accepted her invitation to lunch. She took him to a comfortably furnished eight-roomed house—her own—in which she lived with an aunt whom she supported. For, in addition to the house, Miss Callermere owned an income of six hundred pounds derived from gilt-edged investments.

But these considerations weighed hardly at all with George Muncey—for he had not yet spent fifty pounds of his eight hundred, and at this stage he had certainly no thought of marriage with Miss Callermere.

Neither of them had any occupation, so they could meet whenever they chose. Miss Callermere undertook to show George London. Her father had been a cheery, beery jerry-builder with sporting interests and she had reacted from him into a parched severity of mind. She marched George round the Tower of London, the British Museum and the like, reading aloud extracts from a guide-book. They went neither to the theatres nor to the music-halls, for Miss Callermere thought these frivolous and empty-headed—with the exception of *The Merry Widow*, which she believed to be opera, and therefore cultural. And the extraordinary thing was that George Muncey liked it all.

There can be no doubt that this smug little spinster, some sixteen years older than himself, touched a chord of sympathy in his nature. But she was wholly unable to cater to that part of him that had plastered photographs of public beauties on the walls of his bedroom.

She never went to *The Merry Widow* again, but once or twice he would sneak off to Daly's by himself. *The Merry Widow*, in fact, provided him with a dream-life. We may infer that in his imagination he identified himself with Mr. Joseph Coyne, who nightly, in the character of Prince Dannilo, would disdain the beautiful Sonia only to have her rush the more surely to his arms in the finale. Rather a dangerous fantasy for a backward young man who was beginning to lose his shyness!

There was, indeed, very little shyness about him when, one evening after seeing Miss Callermere home, he was startled by the sight of a young parlor-maid who had been sent out to post a letter some fifty yards from Miss Callermere's house. If she bore little or no likeness to Miss Lily Elsie in the rôle of Sonia, she certainly looked quite lovely in her white cap and the streamers that were then worn. And she was smiling and friendly and natural.

She was, of course, Ethel Fairbrass. She lingered with George Muncey for over five minutes. And then comes another of those strange little dialogues.

"Funny a girl like you being a slavey! When's your evening off?"

"Six o'clock tomorrow. But what's it got to do with you?"

"I'll meet you at the corner of this road. Promise you I will."

"Takes two to make a promise. My name's Ethel Fairbrass, if you want to know. What's yours?"

"Dannilo."

"Coo! Fancy calling you that! Dannilo what?"

George had not foreseen the necessity for inventing a surname and discovered that it is quite difficult. He couldn't very well say "Smith" or "Robinson," so he said:

"Prince."

George, it will be observed, was not an imaginative man. When she met him the following night he could think of nowhere to take her but to *The Merry Widow*. He was even foolish enough to let her have a program, but she did not read the names of the characters. When the curtain went up she was too entranced with Miss Lily Elsie, whom (like every pretty girl at the time) she thought she resembled, to take any notice of Mr. Joseph Coyne and his character name. If she had tumbled to the witless transposition of the names she might have become suspicious of him. In which case George Muncey might have lived to a ripe old age.

But she didn't.

93

Altogether, Ethel Fairbrass proved an extremely satis-factory substitute for the dream-woman of George's fantasy. Life was beginning to sweeten. In the daylight hours he would enjoy his friendship with Miss Callermere, the plea-sure of which was in no way touched by his infatuation for the pretty parlor-maid.

In early September Ethel became entitled to her holiday. She spent the whole fortnight with George at Southend. And George wrote daily to Miss Callermere, telling her that he was filling the place of a chemist friend of his mother's, while the latter took his holiday. He actually contrived to have the letters addressed to the care of a local chemist. The letters were addressed "George Mun-cey" while at the hotel the couple were registerd as "Mr. and Mrs. D. Prince."

Now the fictional Prince Dannilo was notoriously an open-handed and free-living fellow—and Dannilo Prince proceeded to follow in his footsteps. Ethel Fairbrass un-doubtedly had the time of her life. They occupied a suite. ("Coo! A bathroom all to our own two selves and use it whenever we like!")

He hired a car for her, with chauffeur—which cost ten pounds a day at that time. He gave her champagne when-ever he could induce her to drink it and bought her some quite expensive presents.

It is a little surprising that at the end of a fortnight of this kind of thing she went back to her occupation. But she did. There was nothing of the mercenary about Ethel.

On his return to London, George was very glad to see Miss Callermere. They resumed their interminable walks and he went almost daily to her house for lunch or dinner. A valuable arrangement, this, for the little diversion at Southend had made a sizable hole in his eight hundred pounds.

It was a bit of a nuisance to have to leave early in order to snatch a few minutes with Ethel. After Southend the few snatched minutes had somehow lost their charm. There were, too, Ethel's half-days and her Sundays, the latter involving him in a great many troublesome lies to Miss Callermere.

In the middle of October he started sneaking off to *The Merry Widow* again. Which was a bad sign. For it meant that he was turning back again from reality to his dream-life.

The Reality, in the meantime, had lost her high spirits and was inclined to weep unreasonably and to nag more than a little.

At the beginning of November Ethel presented him with certain very valid arguments in favor of fixing the date of their wedding, a matter which hitherto had been kept vaguely in the background. George was by now heartily sick of her and contemplated leaving her in the lurch. Strangely enough, it was her final threat to tell Miss Callermere that turned the scale and decided George to make the best of a bad job and marry her.

As Dannilo Prince he married her one foggy morning at the registrar's office in Henrietta Street. Mr. and Mrs. Fairbrass came up from Banbury for the wedding. They were not very nice about it, although from the social point of view the marriage might be regarded as a step-up for Ethel.

"Where are you going for your honeymoon?" asked Mrs. Fairbrass. "That is—if you're going to *have* a honeymoon?"

"Southend," said the unimaginative George, and to Southend he took her for the second time. There was no need for a suite now, so they went to a small family and commercial hotel. Here George was unreasonably jealous of the commercial travelers, who were merely being polite to a rather forlorn bride. In wretched weather he insisted on taking her for walks, with the result that he himself caught a very bad cold. Eucalyptus and hot toddy became the dominant note in a town which was associated in the girl's mind with champagne and bath salts. But they had to stick it for the full fortnight, because George had told Miss Callermere that he was again acting as substitute for the chemist friend of his mother's in Southend.

According to the files of the Department, they left Southend by the three-fifteen on the thirtieth of November. George had taken first-class returns. The three-fifteen was a popular non-stop, but on this occasion there were hardly a score of persons traveling to London. One of the first-class carriages was occupied by a man alone with a young baby, wrapped in a red shawl. Ethel wanted to get into this compartment, perhaps having a sneaking hope that the man would require her assistance in dealing with the baby. But George did not intend to concern himself with babies one moment before he would be compelled to do so, and they went into another compartment.

Ethel, however, seems to have looked forward to her impending career with a certain pleasure. Before leaving Southend she had paid a visit to one of those shops that cater to summer visitors and miraculously remain open through the winter. She had a bulky parcel, which she opened in the rather pathetic belief that it would amuse George.

The parcel contained a large child's bucket, a disproportionately small wooden spade, a sailing-boat to the scale of the spade, a length of Southend rock and a rubber trumpet of which the stem was wrapped round with red and blue wool. It was a baby's trumpet and of rubber so that it should not hurt the baby's gums. In the mouthpiece, shielded by the rubber, was a little metal contraption that made the noise.

Ethel put the trumpet to her mouth and blew through the metal contraption.

Perhaps, in fancy, she heard her baby doing it. Perhaps, after a honeymoon of neglect and misery, she was making a desperate snatch at the spirit of gaiety, hoping he would attend to her and perhaps indulge in a little horseplay. But for the actual facts we have to depend on George's version.

"I said, 'Don't make that noise, Ethel—I'm trying to read' or something like that. And she said, 'I feel like a bit of music to cheer me up' and she went on blowing the trumpet. So I caught hold of it and threw it out of the window. I didn't hurt her and she didn't seem to mind much. And we didn't have another quarrel over it and I went on reading my paper until we got to London."

At Fenchurch Street they claimed their luggage and left the station. Possibly Ethel abandoned the parcel containing the other toys for they were never heard of again.

When the train was being cleaned, a dead baby was found under the seat of a first-class compartment, wrapped in a red shawl. It was subsequently ascertained that the baby had not been directly murdered but had died more or less naturally in convulsions.

But before this was known, Scotland Yard searched for the man who had been seen to enter the train with the baby, as if for a murderer. A plate-layer found the rubber trumpet on the line and forwarded it to them. They combed the shops of Southend and found that only one rubber trumpet had been sold—to a young woman whom the shopkeeper did not know. The trail ended here.

The rubber trumpet went to the Department of Dead Ends.

* * *

Of the eight hundred pounds there was a little over a hundred and fifty left by the time they returned from the official honeymoon at Southend. He took her to furnished rooms in Ladbroke Grove and a few days later to a tenement in the same district, which he furnished at a cost of thirty pounds.

She seems to have asked him no awkward questions about money. Every morning after breakfast he would leave the tenement, presumably in order to go to work. Actually he would loaf about the West End until it was time to meet Miss Callermere. He liked especially going to the house in Battersea for lunch on Sundays. And here, of course, the previous process reversed itself and it was Ethel who had to be told the troublesome lies that were so difficult to invent.

"You seem different lately, George," said Miss Callermere one Sunday after lunch. "I believe you're living with a ballet girl."

George was not quite sure what a ballet girl was but it sounded rather magnificently wicked. As he was anxious not to involve himself in further inventions, he said:

"She's not a ballet girl. She used to be a parlor-maid."

"I really only want to know one thing about her," said Miss Callermere, "and that is, whether you are fond of her?"

"No, I'm not!" said George with complete truthfulness.

"It's a pity to have that kind of thing in your life—you are dedicated to science. For your own sake, George, why not get rid of her?"

Why not? George wondered why he had not thought of it before. He had only to move, to stop calling himself by the ridiculous name of Dannilo Prince, and the thing was as good as done. He would go back at once and pack.

When he got back to the tenement Ethel gave him an unexpectedly warm reception.

"You told me you were going to the S.D.P. Sunday Brotherhood, you did. And you never went near them, because you met that there Miss Callermere in Battersea Park, because I followed you and saw you. And then you went back to her house, which is Number Fifteen, Laurel Road, which I didn't know before. And what you can see in a dried-up old maid like that beats me. It's time she knew that she's rolling her silly sheep's eyes at another woman's husband. And I'm going to tell her before I'm a day older."

She was whipping on hat and coat and George lurched forward to stop her. His foot caught on a gas-ring, useless now that he had installed a gas-range—a piece of lumber that Ethel ought to have removed weeks ago. But she used it as a stand for the iron.

George picked up the gas-ring. If she were to go to Miss Callermere and make a brawl, he himself would probably never be able to go there again. He pushed her quickly on to the bed, then swung the gas-ring—swung it several times.

He put all the towels, every soft absorbent thing he could find, under the bed. Then he washed himself, packed a suitcase and left the tenement.

He took the suitcase to his old lodgings, announced that he had come back there to live, and then presented himself at the house in Battersea in time for supper.

"I've done what you told me," he said to Miss Callermere. "Paid her off. Shan't hear from her any more."

The Monday morning papers carried the news of the murder, for the police had been called on Sunday evening by the tenants of the flat above. The hunt was started for Dannilo Prince.

99

By Tuesday the dead girl's parents had been interviewed and her life-story appeared on Wednesday morning. "My daughter was married to Prince at the Henrietta Street registrar's office on November 16th, 1907. He took her straight away for a honeymoon at Southend, where they stayed for a fortnight." There was a small crowd at the bottom of Laurel Road to gape at the house where she had so recently worked as a parlor-maid. Fifty yards from Number Fifteen! But if Miss Callermere noticed the crowd she is not recorded as having commented upon it to anyone.

In a few days Scotland Yard knew that they would never find Dannilo Prince. In fact, it had all been as simple as George had anticipated. He had just moved—and that was the end of his unlucky marriage. The addition of the murder had not complicated things because he had left no clue behind him.

Now as there was nothing whatever to connect George Muncey with Dannilo Prince, George's chances of arrest were limited to the chance of an accidental meeting between himself and someone who had known him as Prince. There was a hotel proprietor, a waiter and a chambermaid at Southend and an estate-agent at Ladbroke Grove. And, of course, Ethel's father and mother. Of these persons only the estate-agent lived in London.

A barrister, who was also a statistician, entertained himself by working out the averages. He came to the conclusion that George Muncey's chance of being caught was equal to his chance of winning the first prize in the Calcutta Sweep *twenty-three times in succession.*

But the barrister did not calculate the chances of the illogical guesswork of the Department of Dead Ends hitting the bull's-eye by mistake.

While the hue and cry for Dannilo Prince passed over his head, George Muncey dedicated himself to science with such energy that in a fortnight he had obtained a post with a chemist in Walham. Here he presided over a counter devoted to fancy soaps, hot-water bottles, photographic apparatus and the like—for which he received two pounds a week and a minute commission that added zest to his work.

At Easter he married Miss Callermere in church. That lady had mobilized all her late father's associates and, to their inward amusement, arrayed herself in white satin and veil for the ceremony. As it would have been unreasonable to ask George's employers for a holiday after so short a term of service, the newly married couple dispensed with a honeymoon. The aunt entered a home for indigent gentlewomen with an allowance of a hundred a year from her niece. George once again found himself in a spacious, well-run house.

During their brief married life, this oddly assorted couple seem to have been perfectly happy. The late Mr. Callermere's friends were allowed to slip back into oblivion, because they showed a tendency to giggle whenever George absent-mindedly addressed his wife as "Miss Callermere."

His earnings of two pounds a week may have seemed insignificant beside his wife's unearned income. But in fact it was the basis of their married happiness. Every Saturday he handed her the whole of his wages. She would retain twenty-five shillings, because they both considered it essential to his self-respect that he should pay the cost of his food. She handed him back fifteen shillings for pocket-money. She read the papers and formed his opinions for him. She seemed to allow him little of what most men would regard as pleasure, but George had no complaint on this score.

Spring passed into summer and nearly everybody had forgotten the murder of Ethel Prince in a tenement in Ladbroke Grove. It is probably true to say that, in any real sense of the word, George Muncey had forgotten it too. He had read very little and did not know that murderers were popularly supposed to be haunted by their crime and to start guiltily at every chance mention of it.

He received no reaction whatever when his employer said to him one morning:

"There's this job-line of rubber trumpets. I took half a gross. We'll mark them at one-and-a-penny. Put one on your counter with the rubber teats and try them on women with babies."

George took one of the rubber trumpets from the cardboard case containing the half gross. It had red and blue wool wound about the stem. He put it next the rubber teats and forgot about it.

Wilkins, the other assistant, held his pharmaceutical certificate, but he was not stand-offish on that account. One day, to beguile the boredom of the slack hour after lunch, he picked up the rubber trumpet and blew it.

Instantly George was sitting in the train with Ethel, telling her "not to make that noise." When Wilkins put the trumpet down, George found himself noticing the trumpet and thought the red and blue wool very hideous. He picked it up—Ethel's had felt just like that when he had thrown it out of the window.

Now it cannot for one moment be held that George felt anything in the nature of remorse. The truth was that the rubber trumpet, by reminding him so vividly of Ethel, had stirred up dormant forces in his nature. Ethel had been very comely and jolly and playful when one was in the mood for it—as one often was, in spite of everything.

The trumpet, in short, produced little more than a sense of bewilderment. Why could not things have gone on as they began? It was only as a wife that Ethel was utterly intolerable, because she had no sense of order and did not really look after a chap. Now that he was married to Miss Callermere, if only Ethel had been available on, say, Wednesday evenings and alternate Sundays, life would have been full at once of color and comfort. . . . He tried to sell the trumpet to a lady with a little girl and a probable baby at home, but without success.

On the next day he went as far as admitting to himself that the trumpet had got on his nerves. Between a quarter to one and a quarter past, when Wilkins went out to lunch, he picked up the trumpet and blew it. And just before closing-time he blew it again, when Wilkins was there.

George was not subtle enough to humbug himself. The trumpet stirred longings that were better suppressed. So the next day he wrote out a bill for one-and-a-penny, put one-and-a-penny of his pocket money into the cash register and stuffed the trumpet into his coatpocket. Before supper that night he put it in the hot-water furnace.

"There's a terrible smell in the house. What did you put in the furnace, George?"

"Nothing."

"Tell me the truth, dear."

"A rubber trumpet stuck on my counter. Fair got on my nerves, it did. I paid the one-and-a-penny and I burnt it."

"That was very silly, wasn't it? It'll make you short in your pocket money. And in the circumstances I don't feel inclined to make it up for you."

That would be all right, George assured her, and inwardly thought how lucky he was to have such a wife. She could keep a fellow steady and pull him up when he went one over the odds.

Three days later his employer looked through the stock.

"I see that rubber trumpet has gone. Put up another. It may be a good line."

And so the whole business began over again. George, it will be observed, for all his unimaginativeness, was a spiritually economical man. His happy contentment with his wife would, he knew, be jeopardized if he allowed himself to be reminded of that other disorderly, fascinating side of life that had been presided over by Ethel.

There were six dozen of the rubber trumpets, minus the one burnt at home, and his employer would expect one-and-a-penny for each of them. Thirteen shillings a dozen. But the dozens themselves were thirteen, which complicated the calculation, but in the end he got the sum right. He made sure of this by doing it backwards and "proving" it. He still had twenty-three pounds left out of the eight hundred.

Mrs. Muncey had a rather nice crocodile dressing-case which she had bought for herself and quite falsely described as "gift of the bridegroom to the bride."

On the next day George borrowed the crocodile dressing-case on the plea that he wished to bring some goods from the shop home for Christmas. He brought it into the shop on the plea that it contained his dinner jacket and he intended to change at the house of a friend without going home that night. And as he was known to have married "an heiress" neither Wilkins nor his employer was particularly surprised that he should possess a dinner jacket and a crocodile dressing-case in which to carry it about.

At a quarter to one, when he was again alone in the shop, he crammed half a gross (less one) of rubber trumpets into the crocodile dressing-case. When his employer came back from lunch he said:

"I've got rid of all those rubber trumpets, Mr. Arrowsmith. An old boy came in, said he was to do with an Orphanage, and I talked him into buying the lot."

Mr. Arrowsmith was greatly astonished.

"Bought the lot did you say? Didn't he ask for a discount?"

"No, Mr. Arrowsmith. I think he was a bit loopy myself."

Mr. Arrowsmith looked very hard at George and then at the cash register. Six thirteens, less one, at one-and-a-penny—four pounds, three and fivepence. It was certainly a very funny thing. But then, the freak customer appears from time to time and at the end of the day Mr. Arrowsmith had got over his surprise.

Journeying from Walham to Battersea, one goes on the Underground to Victoria Station, and continues the journey on the overhead electric. From the fact that George Muncey that evening took the crocodile case to Victoria Station, it has been argued that he intended to take the rubber trumpets home and perhaps bury them in the garden or deal with them in some other way. But this ignores the fact that he told his wife he intended to bring home some goods for Christmas.

The point is of minor importance, because the dressing-case never reached home with him that night. At the top of the steps leading from the Underground it was snatched from him.

George's first sensation, on realizing that he had been robbed, was one of relief. The rubber trumpets, he had already found, could not be burnt, would certainly have been a very great nuisance to him. The case, he knew, cost fifteen guineas, and there was still enough left of the twenty-three pounds to buy a new one on the following day.

At closing-time the next day, while George and Wilkins were tidying up, Mr. Arrowsmith was reading the evening paper.

"Here, Muncey! Listen to this. 'Jake Mendel, thirty-seven, of no fixed abode, was charged before Mr. Plowden this morning with the theft of a crocodile dressing-case from the precincts of Victoria Station. Mr. Plowden asked the police what was inside the bag. "A number of toy trumpets, your worship, made of rubber. There were seventy-seven of 'em all told." Mr. Plowden: "Seventy-seven rubber trumpets! Well, *now* there really is no reason why the police should not have their own band." (Laughter.)' "
Mr. Arrowsmith laughed too and then: "Muncey, that looks like your lunatic."

"Yes, Mr. Arrowsmith," said George indifferently, then went contentedly home to receive his wife's expostulations about a new crocodile dressing-case which had been delivered during the afternoon. It was not quite the same to look at, because the original one had been made to order. But it had been bought at the same shop and the manager had obliged George by charging the same price for it.

In the meantime the police were relying on the newspaper paragraph to produce the owner of the crocodile case. When he failed to materialize on the following morning they looked at the name of the manufacturer and took the case round to him.

The manufacturer informed them that he had made that case the previous Spring to the order of a Miss Callermere—that the lady had since married and only that previous day her husband, Mr. Muncey, had ordered an

106

exactly similar one but had accepted a substitute from stock.

"Ring up George Muncey and ask him to come up and identify the case—and take away those India-rubber trumpets!" ordered the Superintendent.

Mrs. Muncey answered the telephone and from her they obtained George's business address.

"A chemist's assistant!" said the Superintendent. "Seems to me rather rum. Those trumpets may be his employer's stock. And he may have been pinching 'em. Don't ring him up—go down. And find out if the employer has anything to say about the stock. See him before you see Muncey."

At Walham the Sergeant was taken into the dispensary where he promptly enquired whether Mr. Arrowsmith had missed seventy-seven rubber trumpets from his stock.

"I haven't missed them—but I sold them the day before yesterday—seventy-seven, that's right! Or rather, my assistant, George Muncey, did. Here, Muncey!" And as George appeared:

"You sold the rest of the stock of those rubber trumpets to a gentleman who said he was connected with an Orphanage—the day before yesterday it was—didn't you?"

"Yes, Mr. Arrowsmith," said George.

"Bought the lot without asking for a discount," said Mr. Arrowsmith proudly. "Four pounds, three shillings and fivepence. I could tell you of another case that happened years ago when a man came into this very shop and—"

The Sergeant felt his head whirling a little. The assistant had sold seventy-seven rubber trumpets to an eccentric gentleman. The goods had been duly paid for and taken away—and the goods were subsequently found in the assistant's wife's dressing-case.

"Did you happen to have a crocodile dressing-case stolen from you at Victoria Station the day before yesterday, Mr. Muncey?" asked the Sergeant.

George was in a quandary. If he admitted that the crocodile case was his wife's—he would admit to Mr. Arrowsmith that he had been lying when he had said that he had cleverly sold the whole of the seventy-seven rubber trumpets without even having to give away a discount. So: "No."

"Ah, I thought not! There's a mistake somewhere. I expect it's that manufacturer put us wrong. Sorry to have troubled you. Good-morning!"

"Wait a minute!" said Mr. Arrowsmith. "You *did* have a crocodile dressing-case here that day, Muncey, with your evening clothes in it. And you do go home by Victoria. But what is that about the trumpets, Sergeant? They couldn't have been in Mr. Muncey's case if he sold them over the counter."

"I don't know what they've got hold of, Mr. Arrowsmith, and that's a fact," said George. "I think I'm wanted in the shop."

George was troubled, so he got leave to go home early. He told his wife how he had lied to the police, and confessed to her about the trumpets. Soon she had made him tell her the real reason for his dislike of the trumpets. The result was that when the police brought her the original crocodile case she flatly denied that it was hers.

In law, there was no means by which the ownership of the case could be foisted upon the Munceys against their will. Pending the trial of Jake Mendel, the pickpocket, the case, with its seventy-seven rubber trumpets, was deposited with the Department of Dead Ends.

A few feet above it on a shelf stood the identical trumpet which George Muncey had thrown out of the window on the three-fifteen, non-stop Southend to Fenchurch Street, some seven months ago.

The Department took one of the trumpets from the bag and set it beside the trumpet on the shelf. There was no logical connection between them whatever. The Department simply guessed that there might be a connection.

They tried to connect Walham with Southend and drew blank. They traced the history of the seventy-seven Walham trumpets and found it simple enough until the moment when George Muncey put them in the crocodile case.

They went back to the Southend trumpet and read in their files that it had not been bought by the man with the baby but by a young woman.

Then they tried a cross-reference to young women and Southend. They found that dead end, the Ethel Fairbrass murder. They found: *"My daughter was married to Prince at the Henrietta Street registrar's office on November the sixteenth, 1907. He took her straight away for a honeymoon at Southend where they stayed a fortnight."*

Fourteen days from November the sixteenth meant November the thirtieth, the day the rubber trumpet was found on the line.

One rubber trumpet is dropped on railway line by (possibly) a young woman. The young woman is subsequently murdered (but not with rubber trumpet). A young man behaves in an eccentric way with seventy-seven rubber trumpets six months later.

The connection was wholly illogical. But the Department specialized in illogical connections. It communicated its wild guess to Detective-Inspector Rason.

Rason went to Banbury and brought the old Fairbrass couple to Walham. He gave them five shillings and sent them into Arrowsmith's to buy a hot-water bottle.

One More Clue

Craig Rice

Craig Rice is among the best of the distaff detective
writers—a wonderful woman who had a store of stories
I have seldom heard equalled. Craig Rice wasn't her
legal name, by the way—as far as can be discovered
at this late date, her name was Craig Georgianna
Craig.

She's best known today for her series of novels
featuring the rumpled and somewhat drunken lawyer-
detective John J. Malone, which have recently been
reissued in paperback—and for a non-Malone detective
novel called Having Wonderful Crime, *the movie
version of which you can find at your local video shop.*

*This story, which may be the oddest of the many,
many who-poisoned-the-drink challenges, was voted
among the best of its year. It may be better than that.*

"**Y**ou've got to believe me," the beautiful girl said. "I had nothing to do with it. I was just as surprised as Arthur—"

She produced a handkerchief from her purse and cried into it, softly. John J. Malone sat behind his desk feeling uncomfortable. "Now, now," he said. The girl went on sobbing. Malone said, "There, there."

"But it's terrible," the girl said at last. "Arthur is dead, and—" She went back to the handkerchief.

Malone sighed. "I'd like to help you," he said untruthfully, "but you'll have to tell me all about it. Now, let's start from the beginning. Your name is Sheila Manson."

The girl stopped sobbing as if someone had thrown a switch. She brushed hair the color of cornsilk away from her tear-stained face, looked up at Malone, and said, "But how did you know?"

Malone didn't think it was worthwhile telling Sheila Manson that a good description of her had been in every Chicago newspaper for the past forty-eight hours. "I have my methods," he said airily, trying to look mysterious.

"Then you must know about Arthur, too," Sheila Manson said.

"Suppose you tell me," Malone suggested diplomatically.

Sheila nodded. She put the handkerchief away in her

purse and said, "He was my fiancé. Arthur Bent. We were going to be married next week."

"And now he's dead," Malone encouraged her sympathetically.

She nodded again. "And the police think I did it, but I didn't. You believe me, don't you, Mr. Malone?"

"Why do the police think you killed your fiancé?" Malone said, side-stepping neatly.

Sheila Manson shook her head. "I don't know why," she said. "But I can tell you who really did kill him."

There was a little silence. At last Malone prodded, "Who?"

"Mae Ammon," Sheila said. "After all, she was right there, too. And if I didn't do it, she must have."

"Mae Ammon?"

"She's just no good," Sheila said. "She would murder anybody if she thought she could get something out of it."

"And what could she get out of murdering Arthur Bent?" Malone asked.

Sheila shrugged. She was beautiful even when she shrugged, Malone thought.

He decided he had to take the case—even if there wasn't any money in it. Even if he owed the telephone company, his landlord, the electric company, and three restaurants. They could wait, but Sheila Manson was the kind of vision that dropped into a man's office once in a lifetime.

"She was just jealous," Sheila said. "I was Arthur's fiancée, and she was jealous."

To Malone it sounded as if Mae Ammon had a better motive for murdering Sheila than for doing away with Arthur. However, this was no time for fine distinctions. "I'll do what I can for you," he said decisively.

"I can't pay you very much—"

113

"Don't you worry your pretty head about that," Malone said. "Just give me your address, so that I can get in touch with you—and then go home and try to relax."

"Mr. Malone." Sheila stood up. Her figure was slim and breathtaking. The last shreds of monetary regret disappeared from the little lawyer's thoughts. "If the police come—what shall I do?"

"Shoot it out," Malone said. Then he caught himself. "Sorry—I must have been thinking of something else. If they come, just call me. I'll be right here, or else my secretary will find me. Now, you just relax and stop worrying."

"All right, Mr. Malone." She started for the door, under the lawyer's breathless scrutiny. At the door she turned. "Malone," she said, and her voice dropped an octave, "I'm—very grateful to you."

The door banged and she was gone.

After a minute Malone wiped the smile guiltily off his face, put on a businesslike frown, and told himself that precious time was passing.

He leaned back in his chair, closed his eyes, and tried hard to think about Arthur Bent.

Of course, he had read about it in the newspapers. Bent had been a rich man—and just recently rich, Malone reminded himself. On his twenty-fifth birthday he had become heir to the Bent fortune, as provided in his father's will. Two weeks later Arthur Bent was dead. He'd been poisoned with arsenic, placed in a rye-and-ginger-ale highball. He had taken this fatal drink in his own home, and no one else had been present except Sheila Manson and Mae Ammon.

But neither the bottle of ginger ale nor the bottle of

expensive rye had been tampered with. The poison had been only in Bent's highball.

It certainly looked as if there were only two possible suspects: Sheila Manson and Mae Ammon. Well, he was working for Sheila Manson, Malone told himself; that meant he had to see Mae Ammon at once.

It was perfectly obvious, when you thought about it, that Mae Ammon had committed the murder. After all, Sheila was a beautiful young girl, and beautiful young girls just didn't do things like that. Or, at any rate, Malone was convinced this one hadn't done it.

Unfortunately for Malone's first theory, Mae Ammon was beautiful too.

Her address was, conveniently, in the Chicago telephone directory. Malone took a cab to the quiet brownstone, walked up the steps, and rang the bell.

The girl who answered the door had short black hair and a figure that made Malone almost stop breathing. She was not slim, like Sheila Manson, but Malone decided that he preferred curvaceous and cuddly brunettes. She wore a dark-green dress that clung to her figure like adhesive tape.

"I'm looking for Mae Ammon," Malone said. "But I'd rather be looking for you."

The girl smiled. "In that case," she said, "you're lucky. I'm Mae Ammon. Come in."

Malone followed her, in a daze, through a hallway and up one flight of dim stairs. "Most of the people who live here work during the day," she said as she pushed open the door of a large bright room. "I'm the only one here, so I answer the bell."

Malone said, "Ah," in an intelligent fashion, and followed her inside. The room was high-ceilinged and sunny. Magazines were scattered everywhere—on the blonde-

115

wood coffee table, over the light-green couch and chairs, piled on the hi-fi and the television set. There was even a large bundle of them stacked on the yellow spread of the single daybed.

"So you're Mae Ammon," Malone said, for lack of anything else to say.

"That's right." She smiled again. "Just put some of the magazines on the floor and sit down. Who are you, by the way?"

Malone took a stack of *Life*s and *Look*s from the couch and sat down. "I'm John J. Malone," he said.

"*The* John J. Malone?" Mae Ammon's face showed surprise.

Malone nodded. "The lawyer, anyway," he said with what he hoped was modesty.

"And you're here about poor Arthur," Mae said. Her smile disappeared. "I hope that woman gets the chair," she burst out. "Killing Arthur—and out of sheer jealousy, that's all it was—just because he was my fiancé—"

Malone said, "Stop."

Mae looked down at him. "Stop?"

"Did you say Arthur Bent was your fiancé?"

"That's right," the girl said.

Malone sighed. Things were getting a little complicated, he realized. "I'd heard that he was Sheila Manson's fiancé," he said cautiously.

"Sheila Manson!" Mae looked around the room suddenly, and saw a china dog lying on the floor. She picked it up and threw it against the wall. Malone ducked. The dog landed over his head with a sharp crash, and little pieces of china drifted down the back of his collar.

"*That's* what I think of Sheila Manson!" Mae said. "I hope she gets the chair! Arthur Bent was my fiancé, and I don't intend to forget it!"

116

Malone rose slowly. "I was only asking," he said mildly.

Mae came over to him and put a hand on his shoulder. "Oh, I wouldn't hurt you," she said. "I don't have anything against you. After all, you know I didn't kill Arthur. Why should I—we were going to be married week after next."

"Sure," Malone said. This didn't seem like the proper time to tell Mae Ammon that he was working for Sheila Manson. But Sheila had said she was going to marry Arthur Bent next week. That gave her a week's priority on Mae Ammon. Malone decided, in a hurry, that he'd better not mention that either.

"I just want to find out the truth," he said.

"Well, you know the truth," Mae said. "It was that hussy Sheila Manson, that's who it was. She slipped poison into his drink and he died. And now she's going to be caught and tried and convicted, and I hope she gets the chair—" She bent down and Malone ducked again. But she was only picking up a magazine. "They sometimes give women the chair," Mae said. "This magazine has some stories—but that's not important. I *want* Sheila Manson to get the chair."

Malone took a deep breath. "Suppose," he said gently, "that she didn't do it."

"But she did," Mae said. "I was there. I know."

"Did you see her actually put poison into his drink?"

"Well," Mae said, "not exactly. But I saw him mix the drink—take out the bottles and everything—take his own little stirrer out of the glass, and then drink it. And if *I* didn't kill him, then *she* must have! We were the only ones there."

Malone nodded. There was, he felt sure, another question he should ask, but he couldn't come up with it. "Was there ice in the drink?" he said at random.

"Of course there was," Mae said. "But the police checked the ice tray. There was no poison in it."

That, Malone thought, eliminated another possibility. But it had been a good idea. "Suppose Sheila Manson didn't murder your—suppose she didn't murder Arthur Bent," he said. "Who else might have had a motive?"

"Everybody loved Arthur," Mae said. "He was a wonderful man."

"Sure," Malone said. "But he was rich. Who's going to inherit his money?"

"I was his fiancée," Mae said. "I'm going to inherit."

"Did he make a will?"

Mae shrugged. She too was beautiful when she shrugged. "I don't know," she said with insouciance.

"How about any close relatives?" Malone said.

"He only had two cousins," Mae said. "Charlie Bent and J. O. Hanlon. They both live in Chicago. But they weren't even at Arthur's place. I tell you, I saw everything. He put in the ice, then the rye, then the ginger ale, then he stirred it all up and drank it—"

"I'll do what I can," Malone said diplomatically.

"I'm sure you will," Mae said. "By the way, why are you asking questions? Are you working with the police? Because I told them all of this—"

"I'm just a friend," Malone lied smoothly. "I'm interested in justice."

"So am I," Mae said. "And justice means giving that hussy the chair."

Well, Malone thought when he arrived at his own office again, there's still J. O. Hanlon and Charlie Bent.

He didn't feel much like seeing them, but somebody had to be the murderer. As things stood, the only suspects were a beautiful blonde and a beautiful brunette. Both, it seemed, had been fiancées of the dead man. And each was

118

convinced the other had committed the murder—unless, Malone thought, they were both awfully good actresses.

But if neither girl had murdered Arthur Bent, Malone thought slowly, then how did he die? The arsenic was in his drink. It wasn't in the bottle of rye or in the bottle of ginger ale. It wasn't, according to Mae Ammon, in the ice cubes. So somebody had put it in the particular glass Arthur had used.

Unless he only used one particular glass—and somebody had painted the inside with arsenic beforehand. You could do that, Malone knew, if you used an arsenic-in-water solution. The poison would dry as a thin film, and dissolve again in any liquid.

Of course, it would make the glass look a little filmy . . .

Malone sighed and reached for the telephone.

Five minutes later he put it down. Von Flanagan had been exceptionally polite and courteous—for von Flanagan, that is. He'd actually told Malone what he wanted to know, and hadn't threatened even once to arrest the little criminal lawyer.

There was no arsenic residue in the glass above the level of the drink.

So the glass hadn't been painted with arsenic.

And that meant that either Mae or Sheila had murdered Arthur Bent.

The only trouble was that Malone was sure neither had.

Of course, the glass might have been painted only at the bottom. Malone wondered if von Flanagan had thought of that, and started to call him back before he realized it wouldn't have made any difference.

"It's a funny thing," von Flanagan had said. "Here's a guy who monograms everything he owns—got his own special monogrammed coasters, for instance. Nobody else uses

119

his coaster. But he didn't monogram the glasses. So there'd be no way for anyone to tell in advance which glass he'd use."

And that, Malone thought, made the cheese even more binding.

He reached for the telephone again.

J. O. Hanlon, it developed, would be right over. He sounded on the telephone like the gruff and overbearing type, and Malone wondered if he were in for more trouble. Charlie Bent, unfortunately, couldn't be reached. His housekeeper said he'd been in Central Africa for the last six months on a safari.

And that's where I should be, Malone told himself sadly.

J. O. Hanlon charged into the office like a bull. Behind him the door slammed shut and rattled. "You wanted to see me?" he asked Malone in a voice that sounded as if it had come from the quarterdeck of the *Bounty*.

"Sit down," Malone said nervously. "And relax."

Hanlon dropped into a chair and stared belligerently across the desk. "What can I do for you?" he roared.

Malone winced. "I'm investigating the death of Arthur Bent—"

"I spoke to the police," Hanlon said. "Told 'em everything. You ask the police about it." He started to rise.

"I'd like to ask just a few questions," Malone said. "This won't take much of your time."

"All right," Hanlon said, and dropped back into the chair with a thud. "Ask away. I'm a fair and reasonable man. Willing to help if I can."

Malone cleared his throat, then said, "I understand you were Arthur's cousin."

"That's correct—mother's side of the family. My mother was Arthur's mother's sister."

Malone tried to work it out in his head and gave up. "Cousin" would have to do. "Do you know if Arthur Bent made a will?" Malone said.

"Told that to the police, too," Hanlon bellowed. "Charlie gets it all—good old Charlie."

"Charlie Bent?"

"Right," Hanlon shouted. "Charlie's in Africa now—hunting or some such foolishness. He'll find out when he gets back."

"Ah," Malone said. Hanlon, then, was motiveless. And that still left only two suspects—neither of whom, Malone assured himself dismally, was guilty. But maybe he could clear up a few of the cloudy points.

"I understand your cousin was engaged," he probed cautiously.

"Engaged?" Hanlon broke into gusts of laughter. Malone sat patiently, waiting for the outbursts to stop. At last Hanlon said, "Those two girls, right? Good game of Arthur's, poor man. Engaged to nobody—but he let the girls *think* he was engaged to them. That's why the three of them met up at his apartment that night—to compare notes."

"They had found out about each other?" Malone said.

"Oversight of Arthur's," Hanlon explained. "They both went to his apartment that night to talk things out with him."

Malone suddenly thought of another question. "How do you know about all this?"

"Me?" Hanlon said. "Been going with one of 'em myself—Arthur took her away. She told me all about it before she went to his apartment."

"Which one?" Malone leaned forward.

"Sheila," Hanlon said. "Good old Sheila. I'm sure she didn't do it. Must have been the other one—what's her name—Mae. Sheila wouldn't do a thing like that."

Malone closed his eyes for a long time. At last they opened. "My advice to you," he said, "is to hire a good lawyer. Me."

"Lawyer?"

"To defend you on a charge of murder," Malone said. "You see, I knew there was something—I knew I'd heard *something* that explained the whole killing. But I had to wait until now, when I saw a motive, to remember it and put all the pieces together."

"You're not making any sense," Hanlon said.

"Wait," Malone promised, "and I will. Hanlon, you murdered your cousin—so you could get your girl back."

"What?" Hanlon bounced up.

Malone said, "Relax. I'm going to defend you. Never lost a client yet."

"But I wasn't even there!" Hanlon exclaimed.

"You didn't have to be. Arthur Bent made the perfect victim—for a clever killer. Each of you had some kind of a motive—both girls, and you, and Charlie. But the girls didn't do it—they'd have killed each other first. And Charlie's in Africa. Arthur Bent monogrammed everything except—for some reason—his drinking glasses."

"They were new—he hadn't got around to having his special monogram put on them," Hanlon said.

"And Mae kept talking about Arthur's own individual little stirrer."

Hanlon began to wilt.

"All right," he said, at last, like a balloon gasping out its final breath. "I painted the arsenic on his stirrer . . . I had to get rid of him—so Sheila would come back to me."

"Don't worry about a thing," Malone said. "And admit nothing to the police. You were overwrought. You didn't know what you were doing."

"What?"

"Of course, my services come high," Malone went on persuasively.

"I'll take care of you, Malone," Hanlon said. "I've got some money of my own . . ."

Malone leaned back with satisfaction. Maybe, he thought, he'd get paid by everybody—each in his, or her, own fashion . . .

Coin
of the Realm
Stanley Ellin

*There is nothing left to say about Stanley Ellin,
novelist, short story writer and often recipient of prizes
from the story contest held annually for many years by
Ellery Queen's Mystery Magazine. His very first story
has established itself as a classic, and "The Specialty
of the House" is still widely available.*

*This story is less familiar, but no less effective. I
can't recall any story by Mr. Ellin that wasn't first
rate, and this one is a very special favorite.*

Among other things, he had learned over the years to wait patiently while his wife made herself ready to go out with him, and under no conditions to distract her from the job being done before the dressing-table mirror. So now he waited patiently at the open window of the hotel room, abstractedly looking down at what seemed to be most of the motor traffic of Paris jammed into the narrow rue Cambon below.

"Walt," Millie said, "I'm ready. Walt, did you hear me? I said I was ready."

He turned to face her and saw she was indeed gleamingly, flawlessly ready, wearing that simple little black number which, to his surprise, had cost him $200. She looked fine in it. Just fine. At 46, Millie was as trim and slim as she had been on her wedding day, and a lot more chic.

"You look like a million," he said, soberly nodding his approval.

Her own expression, as she eyed him from head to foot, was anything but approving.

"I wish I could say the same for you. Is that how you expect to go out? That ridiculous Hawaiian shirt and not even a jacket?"

"It's too hot for a jacket. And we're only going to the Flea Market, for Pete's sake, not the opera."

"Even so. And that camera and that great big camera

bag slung around your neck. And that awful cigar shoved into your mouth. Do you know what you look like?"

"What?"

"An American tourist, that's what. A real corny American tourist."

Walt glanced at the beefy, red-faced, bald-headed image of himself in the full-length mirror on the closet door and unsuccessfully tried to suck in the roll of fat overhanging his belt buckle. No question about it, Millie had spoken the truth, but that was all right with him. Even better than all right.

"I am an American tourist," he protested mildly. "Nothing wrong with letting people know it, is there?"

"Oh, yes, there is. You don't go around like this back home, so there's no reason to go around here like some good-natured hick from the sticks. You can look very impressive when you want to."

"Sure, I can. That's how I get the girls." He gave her a broad, comic wink and was disconcerted when she refused to smile in response. In fact, she was looking downright sullen. She was building up to a real storm, Walt thought uneasily—she had been since breakfast.

"Come on, hon," he said placatingly, "something's eating you, isn't it? What is it?"

"Nothing's eating me."

"Don't hand me that. I'll bet you're still bushed from the plane ride yesterday, aren't you? You know what? If you want to stay here and rest while I tend to this Flea Market expedition by myself—"

"I will not!" Millie's nostrils flared. "And it's some expedition, all right. Hunting up old coins for Ed Lynch's precious collection. We've got three little days in Paris for our whole vacation, and he has the gall—"

So that was it.

"Now, let's leave old Ed out of this," Walt said.

"I wish we could." Millie shook her head ruefully. "Walt, you don't know how much I wish you'd remember you're Ed Lynch's partner, not his errand boy. You hardly ever get away with me like this—a few days in Paris two years ago, a few days in Naples the year before that—but any time you do, there's good old Ed handing you that shopping list for his stupid coin collection."

"Millie, if the man asks me to do him a little favor, I can't turn him down, can I?"

"Why not? And I'm sure he didn't ask any favor, he told you to do it. He just has no manners at all. The way he is, he should have been some kind of gangster, not a businessman."

"Now, Millie—"

"I don't care. All I know is I wish you were partners with anybody else in the whole world but good old Ed."

"Well, I'm not!"

It burst out of him so explosively that Millie gaped at him in astonishment. Then her face crumpled woefully. Quickly Walt crossed the room to her, drew her down to sit beside him on the edge of the bed.

"Ah, come on, hon," he said. "I'm sorry. You know I am, don't you?"

She sniffled a couple of times but managed to hold back the tears. "Maybe."

"No maybes about it. But please be reasonable, Millie. Face the facts. You know everything we've got—and we've got plenty—is only because Ed took me into the plant twenty years ago and taught me the engraving and printing business from A to Z. It doesn't matter how much of a roughneck he is, just look at our balance sheet. A fine home in Scarsdale, a big summer place on the Cape, two cars, a new mink whenever you feel like it—As far as that goes, do you know how much your daughter's wedding cost us?"

"She's your daughter, too. And what difference does it make how much it cost? That doesn't make Ed Lynch any easier to tolerate."

"Twenty thousand dollars, Millie. Twenty thousand dollars in cash. And because of Ed I could sign checks for a dozen weddings like that and never feel it. That's what you have to keep in mind."

She shook her head stubbornly. "You've got a lot of ability. You always did. You could have done just as well with somebody else."

"Done what?" Walt demanded. "I hate to bring up ancient history, but what the hell was I fitted for when I got done winning World War Number Two for the OSS? Superspy, that was me. Some qualifications to offer the boys running the rat-race. A thirty-year-old superspy who could get along in a few foreign languages nobody wanted to hear him talk anyhow. But with enough sense to know that when everyone else in the world is swimming in money he's not going to be any ragpicker. That's where Ed came into the picture, Millie, and one thing you have to admit about him. He didn't just talk big money, he delivered it."

"All right, but please don't get so excited. You know it's bad for you."

"I am not excited. I am only trying to settle this between us once and for all. Maybe I'm old-fashioned, but I say it's not a wife's place to mix into her husband's business. I hate to tell you how many times I've seen trouble between partners just because of that. Ed and I are partners, that's how it is, and there's no use talking about it any more. Is that all right with you?"

Millie shrugged ungraciously.

"Nothing to say?" Walt asked.

"No. Except sometimes I wonder if you aren't more married to Ed Lynch than to me."

"Hardly. But come to think of it——" Walt playfully nudged his wife with his elbow "——it might be tougher getting a divorce from him than from you."

"Well, you're not getting any from me, if that's what you've got on your mind," Millie retorted, and Walt saw with relief that she had decided to forgive him.

He wasted no more time—he got up and helped her to her feet.

"Ready to do some shopping then?" he asked.

"You know I always am," said Millie pertly.

Outside the hotel the doorman asked if he should call a cab for them, but Walt said no, and led the way to the Métro station on the Place de la Concorde.

"The subway?" Millie said in surprise at the stairway.

"Why not? I thought you might like to see how the other half lives for a change."

She gave him a look for that but went along amiably, and, it was plain, thoroughly enjoyed the ride. Her tantrum over, the storm clouds quickly blown away, she was the old Millie again, taking pleasure in something simply because she was sharing it with him, just glad to be with him, her arm tight through his. Married almost 25 years, he thought, but when it came to him she was still like a schoolkid on her first date. That was all right with him— highly gratifying, in fact—but it did raise problems now and then. For instance, it made it just about impossible to tell her that sometimes when they were on these trips abroad he would have preferred to be by himself, away from her company.

Ed Lynch had disagreed with his feeling about it, had insisted that having Millie tagging along with him almost every step of the way was the perfect final touch. The complete American tourist with the cute little wife on his arm chattering to him. But that was Ed for you. A cold-blooded specimen, divorced three times and now on the verge of the fourth, he didn't know what marriage to some-one like Millie could mean. For Ed it was always some pinup girl, as hard-bitten as he was. No wonder Millie hated him and his succession of wives like poison.

At Marcadet-Poissionniers station Walt steered the way through the iron-fenced maze of the transfer point to the train going to Clignancourt at the end of the line. There he and Millie ascended the stairs into the golden, sum-mertime sunlight of Paris and crossed the boulevard to the Flea Market.

They were caught up in a crowd as they entered the market grounds. Tourists with Americans predominating, French family parties, young couples dreamily strolling, arms around each other's waist, as if taking a moonlight walk beside the Seine, but all with an eye out for a bargain. And from what Walt could see as he and Millie were carried along by the throng, there was certainly the stuff here to suit the weirdest tastes.

The market was an endless congeries of roadways and alleyways lined with rickety shacks and stands which dis-played every conceivable kind of second-hand goods from rusty paper clips to the stripped-down chassis of a once magnificent limousine. There was an almost insane quality to the variety of merchandise, Walt discovered. At one point, while Millie stopped to admire a shabby Tiffany lamp hanging over the doorway of one of the shacks, he found himself looking through a shoebox full of browned, water-stained, beautifully engraved party invitations issued by various members of the nineteenth-century French no-bility to each other. It was the engraving that caught his professional eye; it was the kind of meticulous craftsmanship devoted to lettering that was so hard to duplicate today; and it was only on second thought that he wondered who would possibly be interested in buying a collection of decaying party invitations.

Offhand, it would have seemed impossible to find the way to any particular location in that bewildering complex, but Ed Lynch had provided careful directions to the one dealer he had assured Millie she should do business with, and they located the place without too much trouble. Millie had been on the verge of buying the Louis Quatorze escritoire she had long yearned for at the antique shop she frequented on Third Avenue in Manhattan, and it had been Ed who had talked her out of the idea. Bullied her out of it, really. If she and Walt were hopping to Paris for a long week-end, he pointed out, they must make the trip pay off by going to this antique furniture dealer in the Flea Market who, so Ed had heard, gave real value for your money. And, of course, while they were at the Flea Market it would be no trouble for Walt to hunt up some rare coins that Ed wanted for his collection. Trust Ed to plan everything so neatly, like a chess master looking six moves ahead.

But the resentful mood that Millie had been plunged into when she saw through Ed's game was gone now as she wandered among the collection of furniture in the shop, her eyes bright with greed. The proprietor of the shop was a brisk, helpful young woman, as quick and hungry as a piranha. She was so insistently helpful, in fact, that Millie had to draw her husband out of doors to have a private word with him.

"What's our limit?" she asked.

"I guess it depends. Did you see what you want?"

"Yes, there's a couple of stunning pieces to pick from. But I have a feeling she'll ask a fortune for either one of them. I'd like to know how much bargaining I have to do."

"From what Ed said, all you can. Remember he told you to go over every inch of the piece and make sure you're not getting stuck. And not to look like you're interested in buying, whatever you do."

"Can I go as high as five hundred dollars?"

"If you think it's worth it. Just take your time before you sign anything."

"But what about you?" Millie said as he had been sure she would. "You know how itchy you get standing around while I shop."

"I don't have to. I can look around for Ed's coins meanwhile. You can wait for me here. I won't be gone long anyhow."

He left, thankful that she always preferred having him out from underfoot while she was at her haggling, and drifted along the rutted, stony, dirt-surfaced roadway, taking no heed of the crowd of bargain hunters going their way around him, his eyes fixed on the signs marking the owners of the stands he passed. Brument, Fermanter, Duras, Puel, Schmitt, Bayle, Mazel, Piron. Battered furniture, from rusty café chairs to gigantic chests of drawers, seemed to be the stock in trade of all these tradesmen except the last one. While a few articles of furniture could be glimpsed through the open door of C. Piron's ramshackle premises, outside his shanty, instead of a display of the best he had to offer, were only some cartons containing broken bottles. Wine and beer bottles, Walt saw when he went over to take a closer look at them, not one of them undamaged. It made as unappetizing a display as he had seen anywhere in the market.

A man emerged from the shanty and leaned against its doorway to watch Walt make his inspection. Cadaverously thin, hard-featured, cold-eyed, he folded his arms on his chest and stood there in indifferent silence.

Walt turned to him and pointed at the tattered cardboard sign tacked to the wall of the shanty. "Piron?" he asked.

The man admitted to this by an almost imperceptible nod.

"I'm looking for a place to buy some coins," Walt said. "Rare coins. I wondered if you could help me."

"*Je ne comprends pas*," the man said. "Don't understand. Don't speak English."

"Oh, in that case," Walt said amiably, and repeated the words in fluent French.

The man's eyes widened in surprise, then were veiled again.

"Coins," he said. "What kind?"

"American pennies. Old ones. The ones with the Indian head on them."

"What years?"

"1903 and 1904."

"And?"

"And 1906."

"Three, four, six—that's the magic numbers, all right," Piron said. "So you're the one."

"Yes."

"And Mercier got my message through to you, I see. But I thought he'd be bringing back the answer himself."

"No, he's only in charge of distribution around here. I handle the complaints."

"So you had to come all the way from America just to handle mine." The man looked Walt over and smiled broadly, showing a mouthful of gold fillings. "Beautiful," he said. "Just beautiful. Who'd ever suspect it? The way you're made up you look like the biggest innocent to ever hit town. You could walk off with the Louvre under your arm, and the cops wouldn't even give you a second look."

Walt motioned at the throng eddying by. "Do we have to talk about it out here?"

"You're right." Piron gestured him into the shanty, closed the door behind them, and slid its bolt into place. With no window to admit the light, the room was bleakly lit by a single flickering kerosene lamp. Its furnishings, Walt saw, consisted of an old kitchen table and chair, its stock was a few monstrously oversized cabinets, highboys, and armoires ranged around the walls.

"We've got all the privacy we need here," Piron assured him. "Hardly anybody seems to be in the market for broken bottles."

"Very smart."

"It is, if I say so myself. And those pieces of junk you're looking at are all so damn big you'd have to buy a cathedral to put them in. No, you don't have to worry about any customers popping in here while we settle our business. All you have to worry about is making me happy. And you can start by sitting down at that table there and keeping your hands on it."

The man was standing behind him. Walt gingerly turned his head and saw the malevolent-looking little automatic leveled at his back.

"What's that for?" he asked.

"What do you think?" retorted Piron. "After what happened a couple of years ago to the guy who operated over in the Belleville district, I take no chances. I also heard something unpleasant happened to that poor stiff in Naples who got out of line before that. So you sit quiet and don't do anything to make me nervous. If you even want to blow your nose, ask me first."

Walt sat down at the table and rested his hands on it, palms down. He leaned back to give the camera and its accessory case clearance. "You seem to know a lot of things that aren't strictly your business," he said. "I suppose that's what it comes to. We pay, or you sing to the cops."

Piron stood a few feet away from the table, the gun steady in his hand. "That's what it comes to."

"And what do you sing about?" Walt inquired placidly. "A couple of crooks being bumped off? Who would you finger for those jobs? Mercier? I guarantee he's got an alibi for both of them that would make you look silly."

"Sure he has. But maybe I know a lot more about your whole operation than just what happened to those two stiffs. Do I look like the kind of idiot who'd try to put the squeeze on you unless I did?"

"You're bluffing. It's a nice try, but it's only a bluff."

"The hell it is. You want to hear how much I know?"

"If you put that gun away. It's hard to concentrate with a gun shoved in your face."

"That's too bad," Piron said with venom, "but it took me a lot of trouble to get this story together, and I'd hate to be interrupted while I'm telling it. After it's over you can judge just what you're up against and what kind of deal you'll have to make."

"I still say you're bluffing."

"Am I? Then listen to this. For one thing, your stuff is being turned out in some plant in America. A big classy print shop. And you've got a first-class engraver stashed away there doing the plates, a real genius who used to turn out counterfeit for the military during the war that they dumped in Germany and Italy. The records say he's been dead for twenty years, but you and I know better, don't we? We know that fancy print shop is just a front for the jobs he's still turning out in the back room, don't we?"

Walt shrugged. "It's your story," he said.

"And a good one, too, isn't it? Maybe worth plenty more

136

than you figured on paying when you walked in here. Because I also happen to know you're too smart to turn out American counterfeit and stir up trouble at home. No, all these years it's strictly franc notes, and lire, and deutsche marks, and maybe pesetas and pounds, too, all shipped inside those pretty bookbinding jobs to dealers like Mercier here, and the one in Naples, and another one in Berlin, and so on all over the place. And they turn over the stuff to small-timers like me to get rid of at thirty percent of the face value, of which I can keep a lousy five percent. Five percent," Piron said with scathing contempt, "and for taking all the risks. Well, it's not enough. That's what I told Mercier and what I'm telling you now. When you know as much as I do you don't rate as a small-timer any more, and you don't have to settle for small-time pay!"

"What kind of pay did you have in mind?" Walt said.

"Oho!" Piron leered at him in golden-toothed triumph. "So you're singing a different tune now. That's a good joke, all right. You sing sweet or I sing sour."

"You're wasting time. Get to the point."

"I will. I don't like these commission deals where I only get my cut from the stuff I peddle. That means when things are slow I could starve to death here. I want some cash, too. Whenever Mercier hands me a bundle of the stuff I want him to stick a wad of real money in my fist. A big wad."

"How big?"

"Let's do it this way," Piron said coldly. "You name me a figure, and I'll tell you if it makes me happy."

Walt shrugged. "I'll do better than that. I'll make the first payment myself right now. But you'll have to put that gun away. You ought to know you're not scaring me with it. You're not really so stupid you'd want to kill the goose that lays the golden eggs."

"And you can't be sure of that until you've tried me out," jeered Piron, the gun remaining fixed on its target. "Now let's see your money. And it better be government issue, too, none of your pretty art works."

"If that's the way you want to do it," said Walt. He slowly stood up, apparently oblivious of the menacing gun, and pressed the catch of the bulky leather case resting against the roundness of his belly.

"Hold it!" snarled Piron. "What the hell do you think you're doing?"

"The money's in here."

"I'll see for myself. Just stick that thing on the table."

Walt unslung the case from around his neck and placed it on the table. Piron approached it as warily as if it might blow up in his face. He prodded its cover back, his eyes never leaving Walt, and lifted out a sizable roll of franc notes bound with a heavy rubber band. He hefted the roll.

"Not bad," he said. "Not bad at all. How much is it?"

"You'll find out when you count it," Walt said. "But one thing has to be understood. This is what you're on the payroll for from now on, and it's what Mercier will have ready for you when you report to him. But try to put the bite on us for more, and you'll be in real trouble."

"And you know what real trouble is, don't you?" gibed Piron.

"Don't strain yourself being funny. Is it a deal?"

"If this is real money. You can pay off some pigeon in counterfeit, not me."

"All right," Walt said impatiently, "take a look at it. Hold it up to the light and see for yourself."

Piron thrust his gun into his pocket, unsnapped the rubber band from the roll of banknotes, and selected one from the middle of the roll. He held it up to the uncertain light of the kerosene lamp, stretching it tight between his fingers, examining it with the eye of experience.

He had time for only one choked cry when the leather strap of the carrying case was snapped around his neck in a garrote. His hands flailed the air wildly as Walt, leaning back against the edge of the table, a knee planted solidly in the small of the man's back, drew the garrote steadily tighter.

Piron's body arched against the restraining knee until it seemed his spine must crack. The only sound in the room was a strangled wheezing in his chest which finally dwindled into total silence. When Walt released his grip on the garrote, the lifeless body sagged to the floor and lay face up, features distorted and sightless eyes glaring at the ceiling.

Any of the armoires in the place had room in it to store a body with twice Piron's heft. With unflurried efficiency Walt unlocked one, placed Piron's remains in it, and locked it. Carefully he polished its massive key with his handkerchief; then, using the handkerchief as a sling, he tossed the key on top of a highboy in a far corner of the shanty where it landed with a metallic clatter.

That chore attended to, he polished the table top with the handkerchief, reclaimed the banknote from the floor where it had fluttered from Piron's hand, replaced it in the roll of banknotes which he thrust into his pocket. He slung the camera case around his neck and looked the room over to make sure everything was in order. Satisfied it was, he doused the kerosene lamp, slid back the bolt on the door with his elbow, casually walked out of the shanty, and swung the door shut behind him with another thrust of the elbow. Then he joined the crowd in the teeming, sunlit roadway and moved along at its tempo, taking in the sights around him with bland interest.

Millie was still at her haggling in the furniture mart when he got back to it. He could see her inside, volubly addressing its proprietor, and he patiently waited outside the place until she appeared before him, her face glowing.

"It's stunning," she told him eagerly. "It's rosewood and only six hundred dollars and that includes shipping. Walt, you don't mind if it costs a little more than we figured, do you?"

"Not if it's what you want," Walt said.

"You're an angel," Millie said. "You really are." Then she remembered. "What about you? Did you find those coins Ed wanted? Those old pennies?"

"I did. Took care of the deal just the way I was supposed to."

"Old faithful," Millie said teasingly. She squeezed his hand. "But oh, Walt, you really should have seen me take care of that biddy inside. Believe it or not, she started off by asking a thousand!"

"A thousand? Say, that's pretty steep."

"Well, it was your fault," Millie said accusingly. "I'll guarantee she took one good look at you and decided, well, here's some more of those stupid tourists who'll fall for anybody's hard luck story."

"I guess she did," said Walt, apologetically.

Goodbye Hannah

Steve Fisher

Steve Fisher was a popular mystery and suspense
novelist of forty to fifty years ago, some of whose work
was adapted for movies.

   Neither he nor anybody else has ever been in much
better form than in this oddly romantic tough story. I
have no idea why it was never taken up by the movies
—perhaps because Vera Caspary's Laura, a suspense
novel, came first.

   But Fisher doesn't need novel length to make this
one work. It's not easily forgotten.

The captain said: "You've been drinking," and that was all he said about it so Smith thought he couldn't be looking so badly; yet Smith knew it wasn't the whisky —or anyway, not just the whisky—that made him look as if he had been hit in the face with a ton of wet towels. His skin was a grayish-white; and there was that glazed ebony in his eyes; and there were lines coming around his mouth. Oh, he was different, everything about him had changed, it was only that in the gray suit, and the felt hat that was shoved back on his head, and the unlit cigarette which hung in his mouth, he looked *somewhat* the same, so that people hadn't begun yet to really notice.

"Listen, Smitty," the captain went on, "what I called you about was 277, a new one, see? I want you to look at it. It might be Hannah Stevens."

Smith grew rigid with pulse throbbing in his throat, and light flaring in his eyes. He gripped the captain's arm, and the captain looked around and down at where his hand was.

"What's this?"

Smith released the grip and gradually found his voice. "You mean you think you've got Hannah here?"

"Well, we don't know. Suicide, nose dive. Battered head—no face that you can recognize. No other identification, either."

Breathing again, Smith said: "Oh." Then: "Let's have a look at it."

They moved through the morgue along the rows of numbered ice-vaults. The captain was saying: "Since you've got that case you'd know if it was her if anybody would. You know all about her, don't you?"

He said: "Yes, all about her. What kind of perfume she used, and where she got her hair done, and what movie stars she liked the best. I know what time she went to bed every night, and what time she got up. I know what her breakfasts were, I—"

"What are you—her brother?"

"No, I've never seen her. I'd never heard of her until you handed me the case three days ago. She was just another missing person. How many thousands have we every year? She was just a name on a card—"

But he stopped talking suddenly for the captain had turned in front of vault 277 and was pulling it out. It slid like a drawer. Smith's heart was massaging his chest, but he knew he had to look down and he did. There wasn't much of a head left. The hair had been copper. The body had been beautiful and young.

The captain said: "And still they come to New York in droves every year to act or model or write or marry a millionaire. I wish they could see her."

Smith was looking at the body and saying: "It isn't Hannah Stevens."

"It *isn't*?"

"No."

"How can you tell?"

"Hannah had a scar on her little toe. The hair on her legs was lighter, and there was a mole just over her hip."

"Listen, screwball, are you sure about that?"

143

"Yes, I'm sure."

"Okay," the captain said, and he shoved back the drawer. "Another one unidentified, that's all." They started walking back toward the office. "What kind of a dame is this Hannah Stevens?"

Smith was looking straight ahead of him. "She's beautiful," he said. "She's the most beautiful thing that ever walked on the earth. Her parents are worth half a million. She made her debut in Boston three years ago and then her folks moved to Newport and she spent most of her time in New York with the young crowd. I have a dozen pictures of her and so have about six of the town's biggest detective agencies."

"Well, you seem to know as much about her as—"

He held up his hand. "I haven't begun to know anything about her yet. She was engaged to a young man by the name of Ronald Watt. I intend to interview him. After that—"

"Listen," said the captain, "I think you've gone whacky, but it's all right. Just keep your face clean and let me know anything new that develops."

"Okay," said Smith, and he turned the cigarette around so that the dry part was in his mouth now. He moved past the captain and through the door.

He sat in his room with a bottle of rye on the table beside him and a lot of peanut shells scattered across the floor. He sat there with his hands folded, staring at the wall, or past it; and then he got up and did a turn around the room and came back, pouring more rye. Now he fixed his gaze on the dresser where her pictures were lined like a display in front of a motion picture theater. He picked up the first picture and looked at her shining eyes. Someone had told him they were gray and her hair was the color of crystal-clear honey. He saw the strong cleft of her chin, and the thin, yet definite, nose line. He saw her beauty in a radiance that blinded him and he put the picture down and picked up the next.

He kept doing this, going over the pictures one by one, and then going back for another drink of rye. He had long ago ceased trying to reason with himself. He had quit looking at his vision in the mirror and saying: "You're going nuts, Johnny. They're going to come and get up and slap you in a straitjacket if you don't snap out of it." There was no longer comprehension, understanding, or sanity of motive. The pictures, her history, the fragments of things he had learned about her; the odor of her perfume that was on the handkerchief that was in his drawer; the torn stocking that he had picked out of the wastebasket in her apartment; the spilled face powder that he had scooped up and wrapped in tissue paper, all of these things he had of hers, all of the stories he had been told of her; everything secondhand, everything old and used; memories of someone he had never known, told him that he loved her.

At first it had been fascination and this had grown to obsession, and then beyond obsession, beyond all reason. When he tried to sleep he thought he heard what they had said was the rich lilt of her voice; he saw her in a shimmering gold gown, walking and talking and dancing; set against a background of a dazzling cut-glass Fifty-second Street cocktail bar, he saw the honey of hair on her shoulders, and he saw her lift a drink to her lips. . . .

The clangor of the telephone jarred him. He went back to the bed and sat down. He picked up the instrument. "Johnny Smith," he said.

"This is Mrs. Stevens," said a soft, restrained voice. "Hannah's mother."

"Yes, Mrs. Stevens."

"I hope you don't mind—you said I could keep in touch with you. It helps, you know."

"Yes," he said, "I know it does." Then: "Have the private detectives—"

"No trace," Mrs. Stevens said.

There was a silence. . . .

"I see."

Emotion lifted her voice for the first time. "We all loved her so—we all want her back so badly, I can't understand why—"

"I know," said Johnny, quietly.

"I'm sending Ronald Watt over to your hotel," she went on; "you wanted to see him."

"Yes, thanks. It may help."

He talked to her for a moment longer and then hung up. He sat there wondering if Hannah's voice had been something like that—if it had had the same softness?

He put the liquor away and cleaned up the peanuts, after a fashion, brushing them all into one corner; then he got up and straightened his tie. He stuck an unlighted cigarette in his mouth and let it dangle there. Then he went to the window, waiting; he looked down ten stories on Manhattan. All of those lights she had known and loved. Where was she? Why had she gone?

He stood here for some time, and then there was the telephone again.

"Mr. Watt downstairs."

"Send him up."

When Watt tapped on the door Johnny opened it, standing there, the cigarette in his mouth, his eyes flickering. "Come in," he said. He looked after the young man as he walked past him into the room; and then he closed the door, leaning back against it. He stood leaning against the

146

door, not saying anything, watching Ronald Watt. Watt was wearing country tweed but he would have looked better in tails and white tie, Johnny decided; his face in one way seemed weak, and in another showed strong possibilities. He had a high forehead, and brown eyes—bleak now—a drooping, though handsome mouth. His hat was in his hand and a boyish cowlick of hair overhung his forehead. He sat down on the edge of the bed.

"She was engaged to you?"

"You mean Miss Stevens."

"I mean Hannah Stevens," said Johnny.

"Yes, we were engaged." Watt was nervous.

"When did you see her last?"

"On the night before she—she disappeared."

"Explain everything leading up to that. I know after she left you she was seen in two other places alone, at the bars. I know she got in a taxicab and said to the driver: 'Just drift around the park, please,' and that she got out of the cab, in the park, at around Ninety-sixth Street, and that no one, apparently, has seen her since. But tell me up to the point where she left you. *Everything!*"

"Why, there isn't much to tell, Mr. Smith. For a month she'd been avoiding me. I kept calling at her apartment. I kept leaving messages; several times I sat all night in front waiting for her to come in, but she never did. And she wasn't at home. But finally she gave in and saw me twice for lunch—that is, twice in succession, and then she agreed to go to dinner with me. Well, we'd had dinner, and we were drinking cocktails, and everything seemed swell again; she seemed to be her old self, warming up to me, and I thought pretty soon I'd say, 'Honey, let's hurry up and get married. I can't stand being without you.' Then she saw someone pass through the dining room."

"Who?"

"I don't know. I asked her and she laughed and said: 'Only the friend of a friend,' but after that she seemed nervous, and finally she took my hand and looked at me in the way that only she can, Mr. Smith. She said: 'Angel, you're rich and spoiled, and a no-good scoundrel, but I love you. Always remember that, will you? That I love you.' She said that, and then she got up. I thought she would be right back. So I sat there. I sat there for an hour and a half."

"That's the last you saw of her?"

"That's the last," said Watt. He had noticed the pictures of Hannah on the dresser and was looking at them.

Smith said: "Why did she call you a scoundrel, Watt?"

"Just an affectionate term. Nothing—"

"Don't lie, Watt."

Ronald Watt leaped to his feet. "I'm not!"

Johnny grabbed the front of his coat and shoved him back down on the bed. "You are, you little punk and I'm going to wallop the head off of you if you don't tell me the whole truth. I told you I had to know everything. I don't know what's the matter with those private cops you've hired, but to me it's obvious that she disappeared on account of you."

"That's a—"

Johnny slapped him across the mouth. "The sooner you talk, Watt, the better."

"Let me out of here!"

"You're not going to get out, and you're going to talk if I have to kill you."

"Blast you, you let me out," Watt said between clenched teeth, and he rose, shoving against Johnny. Johnny clipped him under the jaw, and then he held him up against the wall and slapped him. When he finally let him drop to the bed Ronald Watt sat there with his face bloody and said:

"I don't know what you want me to tell you. Unless it's why Hannah turned cool toward me in the first place. I was doing a little gambling." He looked up, his face pale now. "Old story, isn't it? My family didn't know, no one did except Hannah and she found out by accident. Well, I got in pretty deeply. Damn deeply. I didn't dare open about it to my father and Nicki said I had my choice. He said welshers, no matter who they were, usually had a bad time of it, if I knew what he meant, and I did. They had *accidents*, maybe playing polo. At least that was the rumor, and I was scared stiff."

"I'll bet," said Johnny.

"So he said I had my choice, either that or—or I could work for him. My family was social and—well, he just wanted a little information now and then and—ah, letters and things I might be able to pick up."

"You mean you were to be the go-between for a blackmail racket that Nicki was running."

"Well—"

"That's what you were. Well, the last mug that did that got made the fall guy when the thing fell through—and landed in prison. But go on."

Watt's face was strained. "What could I do? I pleaded with them, and—as it turned out—"

"I suppose Nicki told you to go home and forget it. To forget you owed him money, that he had reconsidered and decided you were too nice a guy to do work like that."

"No," Watt said, "not exactly that. They let me play again one night. I won back every cent I had lost and more on top of it. So what could Nicki do? He had to let me go. That's why I saw, and still see, no reason for telling it. I never did the work. It was just a proposition, and then I got out of it by—"

149

"—By winning back the money. Fool! You didn't win it back. Nicki *gave* it back to you! Know why?"

"Why?"

"Hannah!"

Ronald Watt stared for a moment, and then his jaw gaped open, and his face turned crimson.

"Now get out," said Johnny. "Get out before I kill you."

When Johnny Smith got outside, it was raining. He ducked across the sidewalk and got into a cab. He slammed the door and mumbled an address, and then he sat staring at the shining streets, and the lights along Broadway, at the streetcars, and buses, at the night clubs, and the big cars pulling up in front of theaters; he sat seeing the rain slap against the window, and hearing the music from the radio, and remembering the words Watt had told him Hannah had said before she left. He remembered that Hannah had taken his hand and said to Watt: "You're a no-good scoundrel, but I love you. Always remember that, will you? That I love you?" He thought of this, and of a song Noel Coward had written: "Mad About the Boy"; and he kept watching the rain on the window of the taxicab.

The cab stopped at an apartment on Ninety-seventh Street near Central Park West, and Johnny got out, looking at the entrance of the building. He walked across and went inside, and showed the elevator man his badge, and put a twenty-dollar bill in his hand, saying: "I want a pass-key, and directions to Nicki Spioni's apartment." He had no trouble at all. The elevator man unlocked the door for him and then beat it.

Johnny stepped inside, closing the door behind him. There were a man and two women in the living room, drinking cocktails, and then Nicki, squat, and hard-faced, came in from the kitchen with a drink in his hand. He saw

150

Johnny and the drink slipped and fell, the glass breaking. He said:

"What is this, mister?"

"Get your friends out, Nicki," Johnny said.

"Listen to him," said Nicki.

"I came about Hannah," Johnny murmured.

Nicki's face changed. "Who are you?"

"I'm a cop."

Nicki looked at his friends and they got up, staring coldly at Johnny but not saying anything. They found their wraps and got out. Johnny locked the door. When he turned around Nicki had a gun in his hand.

"All right, copper, now you can tell me just what kind of a caper this is."

Johnny smiled thinly and put an unlit cigarette in his mouth. "Too bad you weren't at your club tonight. I telephoned, had a couple of federal men go down to look at your books; couple of city cops went along, think they might pick up a little evidence that will send you up for blackmail."

Nicki gulped, his Adam's apple bulging from his throat. "Is this—a pinch?"

"Not this," said Johnny, "the pinch will come later. But not from me."

"Get out of my way then," Nicki said; "I'm getting out of here."

Johnny put the sole of one foot against the door and folded his arms. "You aren't going yet. I have a few questions about Hannah."

Nicki's face muscles flinched. "I don't know anything about her."

"No?"

"No, I don't. And you'd better move, or one of these slugs will move you, and I'll roll you aside."

"You won't shoot," Johnny said. "You're too yellow to shoot anybody, Nicki. You go in for blackmail. You go it the dirty way. But you wouldn't kill anybody. You're too afraid of the chair. We both know that, so you can put the gun down and tell me about Hannah or you'll go to the chair anyway—for *her* murder."

"What do you mean?"

"You were the last one to see her. She got out of a cab at Central Park near Ninety-sixth, and came over here. What happened then?"

"She didn't, she—How do you know what she did?"

"Listen, Nicki, we won't go into that. I just want to know what happened."

The squat man was sweating. He put his gun in his pocket, and mopped his face with a handkerchief. But the sweat came faster then he could wipe if off. There was a wild look in his dark eyes; he raised heavy brows, said:

"What else do you think you know?"

"That you made a bargain with her. She was a pawn for Ronald Watt. What did you tell her you were going to do to Watt?"

Nicki was trembling, he seemed to go all to pieces. He suddenly put his arms up over his face and sat down on the divan; he sat there for a moment, and Johnny stood at the door watching him.

"Somebody told me—about her—" he whispered. His fists were clenched. "I told her I was going to use Watt but if she could get the money he owed it'd be okay. She tried—couldn't get the money. Couldn't explain why she needed thirty thousand dollars. She got an allowance, but I wouldn't take payments on installments from Watt so why from her? Then I—I got that idea—I told her after we'd used Watt awhile we'd kill him. I made her think Watt didn't have a chance, and the little punk didn't. I wouldn't have killed him, that was bluff, but *he* thought I would, and so did she—" He stopped here.

"Go on," Johnny said.

"I told her—if she'd come around—if she'd be regular to me—if she wouldn't see anybody but me for a month and—"

"Never mind the details."

"Well," Nicki went on, "that was all right. It was all right, see. I let her see Watt win back his money. I let her see that he was clear. He told her he'd never gamble again. So she thought—that she had saved his life—or I had, and—"

"So what happened?" said Johnny.

"That's it," Nicki whispered, "that's it. I've wanted to tell somebody." He pounded his chest. "It's been here, up inside me. It's been killing me. She was a good sport. She was the squarest kid that ever lived. Never a peep out of her, do you see? Never a squawk. There was never a finer woman ever lived—" Nicki's hands were in his hair now; it was awful to look at him. "Then do you know what happened—"

"Tell me," said Johnny quietly.

"I fell in love with her. Me, Nicki Spioni, I fell in love with her. I was crazy for her. I wanted to marry her. I told her I'd marry her and go straight—just run my club or go away, out West, to Honolulu, anywhere. I'd give her jewels, money, anything in the world she wanted. But she had all that. All of it. She was no cheap chorus girl. She was no Cinderella model, no ham actress. She had everything, I wasn't giving her a thing, I was taking—taking—"

"I don't want to hear that, I want to know what happened."

"The month ended, and she started seeing Watt again. She was crazy for that yellow rotter. I don't know why. She

153

loved him like I loved her. She ate and slept and dreamed him. There wasn't anything in the world she wouldn't do for him. I had taken her pride, I had taken everything from her, but she thought she could go back to him because it had been his jam, and she had gone to bat. She figured that put them on the same plane, and they could go on and be happy even though she'd never tell him about it.

"I was insane with jealousy. I wanted to kill the guy. I wanted to shoot myself. I was going nuts. I couldn't sleep. I couldn't eat. Just the thought of her with him turned me inside out. But I couldn't do anything. She had kept her bargain and I was supposed to keep mine. I was supposed to but finally I couldn't. I couldn't, see? I cracked, do you get it? Went whacky!

"I found out where she was dining with Watt and sent one of my boys there. He passed the table and gave her a signal. When she went out to meet him he told her I wanted to see her, and double quick, or Watt was going to get bumped. Well, she went to pieces then. She had thought I'd be square, too. Oh, what a fool she was to trust *me*— to think that Nicki Spioni could keep his word!" He sucked in breath.

"Well, she came up here to have it out with me," Nicki went on; "she came up here, and I was blind drunk. She was going to marry Watt and she never wanted to see me again. I did everything to keep her. I cried. I got down on my hands and knees and begged. I crawled on the floor for her. But she wouldn't listen. I kept drinking. The room was spinning in a waltz. All I could hear was her saying: 'No! No! No!' I went out in the kitchen and got a knife and said if I couldn't have her nobody would. I said that, then I changed it and said if she went out I'd cut my throat right there in front of her. I said everything and anything that came to my mind. But she started to go anyway. She started to go, and I tried to stop her, and there was a scuffle. But she got out. I stood there looking at the door and then I came back here to the divan sobbing. Oh, I know men don't cry. But I did, I tell you. Like a damn kid. I fell on the divan crying, tearing out my heart, and then I passed out cold. I haven't seen her since."

"You didn't kill her?"

"No! I loved her! I loved her!" Nicki said.

"But more than that—?"

Nicki looked up, his face strangely white, his voice suddenly quiet. He seemed to be looking past Johnny. Then he slipped to his knees. He looked like nothing human. "One of—the boys—thought he saw her—on Seventy-second Street."

That was all he said, Johnny couldn't make him say another word. When the federal agents came about the tax evasion he was still there on his knees looking as if he had lost his mind. He didn't seem to see them at all. When they led him through the door he leaned on them for support as though the flame that was Hannah had burned his eyes from his sockets, and had taken his soul from his miserable body.

West Seventy-second Street: rain and sleet, night after night. You start at West End Avenue, at the drugstore on the corner and walk up. An apartment here, a hotel there. The corner of Broadway, the subway island, on across, the cigar store, the bank, a fur shop, the automat . . . Up and down . . . Faces, old, young, haggard, painted. Eventually a repetition of faces—the same faces, the same people, up and down . . .

Night after night.

He knew every store by name, he knew every merchant, he had been in every apartment and hotel. Over and over he had said: "Beautiful—the most beautiful creature that

155

ever walked on this earth. Honey-blond hair, about five feet four, carries her shoulders back, has a proud walk. Beautiful, the most beautiful creature . . ." The echo of his descriptions. Laughter. Parties. The Sunday papers on Saturday night. "Her name is Hannah Stevens, she's the most—"

He watched her name fade from the papers as other news crowded out the story of her disappearance. The last news he read was that anyone who discovered Hannah would receive ten thousand dollars reward. He read that and smiled grimly, and kept walking. At night he looked at her pictures, and talked to them. Other cases were piled a foot deep in his file. Missing persons. Family hysteria. Descriptions. Suicides. The click of ice-vaults, in and out. "Is this the man you were looking for?" "Is this the child you lost?" "Is this your mother who wandered off last Tuesday night?"

Everything in a swirl. His mind going—gradually. Hannah dominating every thought. The captain's lectures. "Lay off the drinks, Smith." The sobbing women at the office, the laughing husband. "My wife just disappeared." The cranks: "I'm going to commit suicide, so don't look for me!" The captain again: "Now, Smith, you've *got* to find this one, she's probably right over the bridge in Brooklyn; didn't she have a boy friend who—"

But the nights were his own. Seventy-second Street. Up and down, heavy steps, nodding to the merchants.

He saw her on Saturday of the sixth week.

He had been in a market looking for her when she brushed by him and he caught the odor of the perfume and the powder, though it seemed heavier than he had imagined Hannah would use, and he turned to see her back, to see her moving off down the street. He stood watching, trembling, petrified. He had not seen her face

156

and yet he knew that it was she. He knew her better than she knew herself.

He began following, watching the even swing of her legs. He ran a little to catch up, and he heard the click of her high heels on the sidewalk. She walked down to Riverside Drive and turned right. In a moment she entered an old apartment building. He hurried now to stop her, but the door clicked shut, and locked, and she went on in, through the inside door. He had seen no more than her back, the honey color of her hair, but he knew it was she.

He waited there, hearing the traffic on Riverside Drive, seeing the lights on the Parkway beside the Hudson. He had always known, had always been certain that some day he would find her, but now that he had he could not diagnose his emotion beyond a feeling of great triumph. To see her, to talk to her in the flesh, not to her picture.

He climbed the steps of the apartment and scanned the names under the bells. Her name was not there, but she had changed it, of course. He rang the manager's bell. It buzzed and he went in and stood in a dimly lit hall. A fat woman clad in calico waddled out and looked him over.

"Can you tell me where I can find a blond girl who lives here. She's the most beautiful creature that—"

"Upstairs, first door on your right. Only blond we have in the house."

"Thank you," he said. "Thank you." He hurried up the stairs, making a lot of noise, and then he stood in front of her door. In front of Hannah Stevens' apartment. A door opened down the hall and a young woman clad in a kimono looked at him. She kept standing there. He looked the other way, and then another door opened. He did not glance toward it. Hannah's door opened finally. She was there, there in front of him. Her cheeks were rouged, and she was dressed in a red kimono.

She smiled woodenly. "Come in, honey," she said.

But he stood there, staring at her, and at a jagged knife scar that was slantwise across her cheek. It was puffed and red and made her look ugly. Words tumbled through his mind. "I had the knife and I told her I was going to stab myself, but she tried to go anyway, and there was a scuffle. . . . One of the boys saw her on Seventy-second Street. . . ." He remembered these words, looking at her, into her gray eyes, at her honey-colored hair; then he remembered farther back than that, the last thing she had said to Ronald Watt: "You're rich, and spoiled, and a no-good scoundrel, but I love you. Always remember that, will you? That I love you."

"Well, are you coming in or not?"

"No, it—it was a mistake."

He fled down the steps like a fool, rockets exploding in his temples.

At the corner of Seventy-second and West End Avenue he went into the drugstore and telephoned.

"Listen, Captain," he said, "remember that old case— Hannah Stevens? Well, I've found out that I was all wet. Yeah—isn't that funny? I was screwy. First time in my life. I just found out tonight. She was the corpse in ice-vault 277—that one with the battered head—"

When he hung up the telephone, he whispered: "Good-bye, Hannah," and then he put an unlighted cigarette in his mouth and got up and left the booth. He walked briskly toward Broadway.

Three O'Clock

Cornell Woolrich

Cornell Woolrich is the author of many classic suspense
novels, and of a gleaming array of equally classic
short stories. He can generate more suspense than most
writers dream of, and more than a few readers can
comfortably stand.

One of his short stories, "Rear Window," was made
into the classic Hitchcock film. "Three O'Clock" has
been adapted for radio and for TV since its original
publication—and it is the most un-put-downable story
I know. Don't start it if you have anything urgent to
do.

She had signed her own death-warrant. He kept telling himself over and over that he was not to blame, she had brought it on herself. He had never seen the man. He knew there was one. He had known for six weeks now. Little things had told him. One day he came home and there was a cigar-butt in an ashtray, still moist at one end, still warm at the other. There were gasoline-drippings on the asphalt in front of their house, and they didn't own a car. And it wouldn't be a delivery-vehicle, because the drippings showed it had stood there a long time, an hour or more. And once he had actually glimpsed it, just rounding the far corner as he got off the bus two blocks down the other way. A second-hand Ford. She was often very flustered when he came home, hardly seemed to know what she was doing or saying at all.

He pretended not to see any of these things; he was that type of man, Stapp, he didn't bring his hates or grudges out into the open where they had a chance to heal. He nursed them in the darkness of his mind. That's a dangerous kind of a man.

If he had been honest with himself, he would have had to admit that this mysterious afternoon caller was just the excuse he gave himself, that he'd daydreamed of getting rid of her long before there was any reason to, that there had been something in him for years past now urging Kill,

kill, kill. Maybe ever since that time he'd been treated at the hospital for a concussion.

He didn't have any of the usual excuses. She had no money of her own, he hadn't insured her, he stood to gain nothing by getting rid of her. There was no other woman he meant to replace her with. She didn't nag and quarrel with him. She was a docile, tractable sort of wife. But this thing in his brain kept whispering Kill, kill, kill. He'd fought it down until six weeks ago, more from fear and a sense of self-preservation than from compunction. The discovery that there was some stranger calling on her in the afternoons when he was away, was all that had been needed to unleash it in all its hydra-headed ferocity. And the thought that he would be killing two instead of just one, now, was an added incentive.

So every afternoon for six weeks now when he came home from his shop, he had brought little things with him. Very little things, that were so harmless, so inoffensive, in themselves that no one, even had they seen them, could have guessed—Fine little strands of copper wire such as he sometimes used in his watch-repairing. And each time a very little package containing a substance that—well, an explosives expert might have recognized, but no one else. There was just enough in each one of those packages, if ignited, to go Fffft! and flare up like flashlight-powder does. Loose like that it couldn't hurt you, only burn your skin of course if you got too near it. But wadded tightly into cells, in what had formerly been a soap-box down in the basement, compressed to within an inch of its life the way he had it, the whole accumulated thirty-six-days worth of it (for he hadn't brought any home on Sundays)—that would be a different story. They'd never know. There wouldn't be enough left of the flimsy house for them to go

161

by. Sewer-gas they'd think, or a pocket of natural gas in the ground somewhere around under them. Something like that had happened over on the other side of town two years ago, only not as bad of course. That had given him the idea originally.

He'd brought home batteries too, the ordinary dry-cell kind. Just two of them, one at a time. As far as the substance itself was concerned, where he got it was his business. No one would ever know where he got it. That was the beauty of getting such a little at a time like that. It wasn't even missed where he got it from. She didn't ask him what was in these little packages, because she didn't even see them, he had them in his pocket each time. (And of course he didn't smoke coming home.) But even if she had seen them, she probably wouldn't have asked him. She wasn't the nosey kind that asked questions, she would have thought it was watch-parts, maybe, that he brought home to work over at night or something. And then too she was so rattled and flustered herself these days, trying to cover up the fact that she'd had a caller, that he could have brought in a grandfather-clock under his arm and she probably wouldn't have noticed it.

Well, so much the worse for her. Death was spinning its web beneath her busy feet as they bustled obviously back and forth in those ground-floor rooms. He'd be in his shop tinkering with watch-parts and the phone would ring. "Mr. Stapp, Mr. Stapp, your house has just been demolished by a blast!"

A slight concussion of the brain simplifies matters so beautifully.

He knew she didn't intend running off with this unknown stranger, and at first he had wondered why not. But by now he thought he had arrived at a satisfactory answer. It was that he, Stapp, was working, and the other man evi-

162

dently wasn't, wouldn't be able to provide for her if she left with him. That must be it, what other reason could there be? She wanted to have her cake and eat it too.

So that was all he was good for, was it, to keep a roof over her head? Well, he was going to lift that roof sky-high, blow it to smithereens!

He didn't really want her to run off, anyway, that wouldn't have satisfied this thing within him that cried Kill, kill, kill. It wanted to *get* the two of them, and nothing short of that would do. And if he and she had had a five-year-old kid, say, he would have included the kid in the holocaust too, although a kid that age obviously couldn't be guilty of anything. A doctor would have known what to make of this, and would have phoned a hospital in a hurry. But unfortunately doctors aren't mind-readers and people don't go around with their thoughts placarded on sandwich-boards.

The last little package had been brought in two days ago. The box had all it could hold now. Twice as much as was necessary to blow up the house. Enough to break every window for a radius of blocks—only there were hardly any, they were in an isolated location. And that fact gave him a paradoxical feeling of virtue, as though he were doing a good deed; he was destroying his own but he wasn't endangering anybody else's home. The wires were in place, the batteries that would give off the necessary spark were attached. All that was necessary now was the final adjustment, the hook-up, and then—

Kill, kill, kill, the thing within him gloated.

Today was the day.

He had been working over the alarm-clock all morning to the exclusion of everything else. It was only a dollar-and-a-half alarm, but he'd given it more loving care than someone's Swiss-movement pocket-watch or platinum and

163

diamond wristwatch. Taking it apart, cleaning it, oiling it, adjusting it, putting it together again, so that there was no slightest possibility of it failing him, of it not playing its part, of it stopping or jamming or anything else. That was one good thing about being your own boss, operating your own shop, there was no one over you to tell you what to do and what not to do. And he didn't have an apprentice or helper in the shop, either, to notice this peculiar absorption in a mere alarm-clock and tell someone about it later.

Other days he came home from work at five. This mysterious caller, this intruder, must be there from about two-thirty or three until shortly before she expected him. One afternoon it had started to drizzle at about a quarter to three, and when he turned in his doorway over two hours later there was still a large dry patch on the asphalt out before their house, just beginning to blacken over with the fine misty precipitation that was still falling. That was how he knew the time of her treachery so well.

He could, of course, if he'd wanted to bring the thing out into the open, simply have come an unexpected hour earlier any afternoon during those six weeks, and confronted them face to face. But he preferred the way of guile and murderous revenge; they might have had some explanation to offer that would weaken his purpose, rob him of his excuse to do the thing he craved. And he knew her so well, that in his secret heart he feared she would have one if he once gave her a chance to offer it. Feared was the right word. He wanted to do this thing. He wasn't interested in a showdown, he was interested in a pay-off. This artificially-nurtured grievance had brought the poison in his system to a head, that was all. Without it it might have remained latent for another five years, but it would have erupted sooner or later anyway.

He knew the hours of her domestic routine so well that it was the simplest matter in the world for him to return to the house on his errand at a time when she would not be there. She did her cleaning in the morning. Then she had the impromptu morsel that she called lunch. Then she went out, in the early afternoon, and did her marketing for their evening meal. They had a phone in the house but she never ordered over it; she liked, she often told him, to see what she was getting, otherwise the tradespeople simply foisted whatever they chose on you, at their own prices. So from one until two was the time for him to do it, and be sure of getting away again unobserved afterwards.

At twelve-thirty sharp he wrapped up the alarm-clock in ordinary brown paper, tucked it under his arm, and left his shop. He left it every day at this same time to go to his own lunch. He would be a little longer getting back today, that was all. He locked the door carefully after him, of course; no use taking chances, he had too many valuable watches in there under repair and observation.

He boarded the bus at the corner below, just like he did every day when he was really going home for the night. There was no danger of being recognized or identified by any bus-driver or fellow-passenger or anything like that, this was too big a city. Hundreds of people used these busses night and day. The drivers didn't even glance up at you when you paid your fare, deftly made change for you backhand by their sense of touch on the coin you gave them alone. The bus was practically empty, no one was going out his way at this hour of the day.

He got off at his usual stop, three interminable suburban blocks away from where he lived, which was why his house had not been a particularly good investment when he bought it and no others had been put up around it afterwards. But it had its compensations on such a day as this. There were

165

no neighbors to glimpse him returning to it at this unusual hour, from their windows, and remember that fact afterwards. The first of the three blocks he had to walk had a row of taxpayers on it, one-story store-fronts. The next two were absolutely vacant from corner to corner, just a panel of advertising billboards on both sides, with their gallery of friendly people that beamed on him each day twice a day. Incurable optimists these people were; even today when they were going to be shattered and splintered they continued to grin and smirk their counsel and messages of cheer. The perspiring bald-headed fat man about to quaff some non-alcoholic beverage. "The pause that refreshes!" The grinning colored laundress hanging up wash. "No ma'am, I just uses a little Oxydol." The farmwife at the rural telephone sniggering over her shoulder: "Still talking about their new Ford 8!" They'd be tatters and kindling in two hours from now, and they didn't have sense enough to get down off there and hurry away.

"You'll wish you had," he whispered darkly as he passed by beneath them, clock under arm.

But the point was, that if ever a man walked three "city" blocks in broad daylight unseen by the human eye, he did that now. He turned in the short cement walk when he came to his house at last, pulled back the screen door, put his latchkey into the wooden inner door and let himself in. She wasn't home, of course; he'd known she wouldn't be, or he wouldn't have come back like this.

He closed the door again after him, moved forward into the blue twilight-dimness of the inside of the house. It seemed like that at first after the glare of the street. She had the green shades down three-quarters of the way on all the windows to keep it cool until she came back. He didn't take his hat off or anything, he wasn't staying. Particularly after he once set this clock he was carrying in motion. In fact it was going to be a creepy feeling even walking back those three blocks to the bus-stop and standing waiting for the bus to take him downtown again, knowing all the time something was going *tick-tock, tick-tock* in the stillness back here, even though it wouldn't happen for a couple of hours yet.

He went directly to the door leading down to the basement. It was a good stout wooden door. He passed through it, closed it behind him, and went down the bare brick steps to the basement-floor. In the winter, of course, she'd had to come down here occasionally to regulate the oil-burner while he was away, but after the fifteenth of April no one but himself ever came down here at any time, and it was now long past the fifteenth of April.

She hadn't even known that he'd come down, at that. He'd slipped down each night for a few minutes while she was in the kitchen doing the dishes, and by the time she got through and came out, he was upstairs again behind his newspaper. It didn't take long to add the contents of each successive little package to what was already in the box. The wiring had taken more time, but he'd gotten that done one night when she'd gone out to the movies (So she'd said—and then had been very vague about what the picture was she'd seen, but he hadn't pressed her.).

The basement was provided with a light-bulb over the stairs, but it wasn't necessary to use it except at night; daylight was admitted through a horizontal slit of window that on the outside was flush with the ground, but on the inside was up directly under the basement-ceiling. The glass was wire-meshed for protection and so cloudy with lack of attention as to be nearly opaque.

The box, that was no longer merely a box now but an infernal machine, was standing over against the wall, to one side of the oil-burner. He didn't dare shift it about

167

any more now that it was wired and the batteries inserted. He went over to it and squatted down on his heels before it, and put his hand on it with a sort of loving gesture. He was proud of it, prouder than of any fine watch he'd ever repaired or reconstructed. A watch, after all, was inanimate. This was going to become animate in a few more minutes, maybe diabolically so, but animate just the same. It was like—giving birth.

He unwrapped the clock and spread out the few necessary small implements he'd brought with him from the shop on the floor beside him. Two fine copper wires were sticking stiffly out of a small hole he'd bored in the box, in readiness, like the antennae of some kind of insect. Through them death would go in.

He wound the clock up first, for he couldn't safely do that once it was connected. He wound it up to within an inch of its life, with a professionally deft economy of wrist-motion. Not for nothing was he a watch-repairer. It must have sounded ominous down in that hushed basement, to hear that *crick-craaaack, crick-craaaack*, that so-domestic sound that denotes going to bed, peace, slumber, security; that this time denoted approaching annihilation. It would have if there'd been any listener. There wasn't any but himself. It didn't sound ominous to him, it sounded delicious.

He set the alarm for three. But there was a difference now. Instead of just setting off a harmless bell when the hour hand reached three and the minute hand reached twelve, the wires attached to it leading to the batteries would set off a spark. A single, tiny, evanescent spark— that was all. And when that happened, all the way downtown where his shop was, the showcase would vibrate, and maybe one or two of the more delicate watch-mechanisms would stop. And people on the streets would stop and ask one another: "What was that?"

They probably wouldn't even be able to tell definitely, afterwards, that there'd been anyone else beside herself in the house at the time. They'd know that she'd been there only by a process of elimination; she wouldn't be anywhere else afterwards. They'd know that the house had been there only by the hole in the ground and the litter around.

He wondered why more people didn't do things like this; they didn't know what they were missing. Probably not clever enough to be able to make the things themselves, that was why.

When he'd set the clock itself by his own pocket-watch—1:15—he pried the back off it. He'd already bored a little hole through this at his shop. Carefully he guided the antenna-like wires through it, more carefully still he fastened them to the necessary parts of the mechanism without letting a tremor course along them. It was highly dangerous but his hands didn't play him false, they were too skilled at this sort of thing. It wasn't vital to reattach the back to the clock, the result would be the same if it stood open or closed, but he did that too, to give the sense of completion to the job that his craftsman's soul found necessary. When he had done with it, it stood there on the floor, as if placed there at random up against an innocent-looking copper-lidded soapbox, ticking away. Ten minutes had gone by since he had come down here. One hour and forty minutes were still to go by.

Death was on the wing.

He stood up and looked down at his work. He nodded. He retreated a step across the basement floor, still looking down, and nodded again, as if the slight perspective gained only enhanced it. He went over to the foot of the stairs leading up, and stopped once more and looked over. He had very good eyes. He could see the exact minute-notches on the dial all the way over where he now was. One had just gone by.

He smiled a little and went on up the stairs, not furtively or fearfully but like a man does in his own house, with an unhurried air of ownership, head up, shoulders back, tread firm.

He hadn't heard a sound over his head while he was down there, and you could hear sounds quite easily through the thin flooring, he knew that by experience. Even the opening and closing of doors above could be heard down here, certainly the footsteps of anyone walking about in the ground-floor rooms if they bore down with their normal weight. And when they stood above certain spots and spoke, the sound of the voices and even what was said came through clearly, due to some trick of acoustics. He'd heard Lowell Thomas clearly, on the radio, while he was down here several times.

That was why he was all the more unprepared, as he opened the basement door and stepped out into the ground-floor hall, to hear a soft tread somewhere up above, on the second floor. A single, solitary footfall, separate, disconnected, like Robinson Crusoe's footprint. He stood stock-still a moment, listening tensely, thinking—hoping, rather, he'd been mistaken. But he hadn't. The slur of a bureau-drawer being drawn open or closed reached him, and then a faint tinkling sound as though something had lightly struck one of the glass toilet-articles on Fran's dresser.

Who else could it be but she? And yet there was a stealth to these vague disconnected noises that didn't sound like her. He would have heard her come in; her high heels usually exploded along the hardwood floors like little fire-crackers.

Some sixth sense made him turn suddenly and look behind him, toward the dining-room, and he was just in time to see a man, half-crouched, shoulders bunched forward, creeping up on him. He was still a few yards away, beyond the dining-room threshold, but before Stapp could do more than drop open his mouth with reflex astonishment, he had closed in on him, caught him brutally by the throat with one hand, flung him back against the wall, and pinned him there.

"What are you doing here?" Stapp managed to gasp out.

"Hey, Bill, somebody *is* home!" the man called out guardedly. Then he struck out at him, hit him a stunning blow on the side of the head with his free hand. Stapp didn't reel because the wall was at the back of his head, that gave him back the blow doubly, and his senses dulled into a whirling flux for a minute.

Before they had cleared again, a second man had leaped down off the stairs from one of the rooms above, in the act of finishing cramming something into his pocket.

"You know what to do, hurry up!" the first one ordered. "Get me something to tie him with and let's get out of here!"

"For God's sake, don't tie—!" Stapp managed to articulate through the strangling grip on his windpipe. The rest of it was lost in a blur of frenzied struggle on his part, flailing out with his legs, clawing at his own throat to free it. He wasn't fighting the man off, he was only trying to tear that throttling impediment off long enough to get out what he had to tell them, but his assailant couldn't tell the difference. He struck him savagely a second and third time, and Stapp went limp there against the wall without altogether losing consciousness.

171

The second one had come back already with a rope, it looked like Fran's clothesline from the kitchen, that she used on Mondays. Stapp, head falling forward dazedly upon the pinioning arm that still had him by the jugular, was dimly aware of this going around and around him, crisscross, in and out, legs and body and arms.

"Don't—" he panted. His mouth was suddenly nearly torn in two, and a large handkerchief or rag was thrust in, effectively silencing all further sound. Then they whipped something around outside of that, to keep it in, and fastened it behind his head. His senses were clearing again, now that it was too late.

"Fighter, huh?" one of them muttered grimly. "What's he protecting? The place is a lemon, there's nothing in it."

Stapp felt a hand spade into his vest-pocket, take his watch out. Then into his trouser-pocket and remove the little change he had on.

"Where'll we put him?"

"Leave him where he is."

"Naw. I did my last stretch just on account of leaving a guy in the open where he could put a squad-car on my tail too quick; they nabbed me a block away. Let's shove him back down in there where he was."

This brought on a new spasm, almost epileptic in its violence. He squirmed and writhed and shook his head back and forth. They had picked him up between them now, head and feet, kicked the basement door open, and were carrying him down the steps to the bottom. They still couldn't be made to understand that he wasn't resisting, that he wouldn't call the police, that he wouldn't lift a finger to have them apprehended—if they'd only let him get out of here, *with* them.

"This is more like it," one said, as they deposited him

on the floor. "Whoever lives in the house with him won't find him so quick——"

Stapp started to roll his head back and forth on the floor like something demented, toward the clock, then toward them, toward the clock, toward them. But so fast that it finally lost all possible meaning, even if it would have had any for them in the first place, and it wouldn't have of course. They still thought he was trying to free himself in unconquerable opposition.

"Look at that!" one of them jeered. "Did you ever see anyone like him in your life?" He backed his arm threateningly at the wriggling form. "I'll give you one that'll hold you for good, if you don't cut it out!"

"Tie him up to that pipe over there in the corner," his companion suggested, "or he'll wear himself out rolling all over the place." They dragged him backwards along the floor and lashed him in a sitting position, legs out before him, with an added length of rope that had been coiled in the basement.

Then they brushed their hands ostentatiously and started up the basement stairs again, one behind the other, breathing hard from the struggle they'd had with him. "Pick up what we got and let's blow," one muttered. "We'll have to pull another one tonight—and this time you let *me* do the picking!"

"It looked like the berries," his mate alibied. "No one home, and standing way off by itself like it is."

A peculiar sound like the low simmering of a tea-kettle or the mewing of a newborn kitten left out in the rain to die came percolating thinly through the gag in Stapp's mouth. His vocal cords were strained to bursting with the effort it was costing him to make even that slight sound. His eyes were round and staring, fastened on them in horror and imploring.

173

They saw the look as they went on up, but couldn't read it. It might have been just the physical effort of trying to burst his bonds, it might have been rage and threatened retribution, for all they knew.

The first passed obliviously through the basement doorway and passed from sight. The second stopped halfway to the top of the stairs and glanced complacently back at him—the way he himself had looked back at his own handiwork just now, short minutes ago.

"Take it easy," he jeered, "relax. I used to be a sailor. You'll never get out of *them* knots, buddy."

Stapp swiveled his skull desperately, threw his eyes at the clock one last time. They almost started out of their sockets, he put such physical effort into the look.

This time the man got it finally, but got it wrong. He flung his arm at him derisively. "Trying to tell me you got a date? Oh no you haven't, you only think you have! Whadda you care what time it is, *you*'re not going any place!"

And then with the horrible slowness of a nightmare— though it only seemed that way, for he resumed his ascent fairly briskly—his head went out through the doorway, his shoulders followed, his waist next. Now even optical communication was cut off between them, and if only Stapp had had a minute more he might have made him understand! There was only one backthrust foot left in sight now, poised on the topmost basement step to take flight. Stapp's eyes were on it as though their burning plea could hold it back. The heel lifted up, it rose, trailed through after the rest of the man, was gone.

Stapp heaved himself so violently, as if to go after it by sheer will-power, that for a moment his whole body was a distended bow, clear of the floor from shoulders to heels. Then he fell flat again with a muffled thud, and a little

174

dust came out from under him, and a half-dozen little separate skeins of sweat started down his face at one time, crossing and intercrossing as they coursed. The basement door ebbed back into its frame and the latch dropped into its socket with a minor click that to him was like the crack of doom.

In the silence now, above the surge of his own tidal breathing that came and went like surf upon a shoreline, was the counterpoint of the clock. Tick-tick, tick-tick, tick-tick, tick-tick.

For a moment or two longer he drew what consolation he could from the knowledge of their continued presence above him. An occasional stealthy footfall here and there, never more than one in succession, for they moved with marvelous dexterity, they must have had a lot of practice in breaking and entering. They were very cautious walkers from long habit even when there was no further need for it. A single remark filtered through, from somewhere near the back door. "All set? Let's take it this way." The creak of a hinge, and then the horrid finality of a door closing after them, the back door, which Fran may have forgotten to lock and by which they had presumably entered in the first place; and then they were gone.

And with them went his only link with the outside world. They were the only two people in the whole city who knew where he was at this moment. No one else, not a living soul, knew where to find him. Nor what would happen to him if he wasn't found and gotten out of here by three o'clock. It was twenty-five to two now. His discovery of their presence, the fight, their trussing him up with the rope, and their final unhurried departure, had all taken place within fifteen minutes.

It went tick-tick, tick-tock; tick-tick, tick-tock, so rhythmically, so remorselessly, so *fast*.

An hour and twenty-five minutes left. Eighty-five minutes left. How long that could seem if you were waiting for someone on a corner, under an umbrella, in the rain— like he had once waited for Fran outside the office where she worked before they were married, only to find that she'd been taken ill and gone home early that day. How long that could seem if you were stretched out on a hospital-bed with knife-pains in your head and nothing to look at but white walls, until they brought your next tray—as he had been that time of the concussion. How long that could seem when you'd finished the paper, and one of the tubes had burned out in the radio, and it was too early to go to bed yet. How short, how fleeting, how instantaneous, that could seem when it was all the time there was left for you to live in and you were going to die at the end of it!

No clock had ever gone this fast, of all the hundreds that he'd looked at and set right. This was a demon-clock, its quarter-hours were minutes and its minutes seconds. Its lesser hand didn't even pause at all on those notches the way it should have, passed on from one to the next in perpetual motion. It was cheating him, it wasn't keeping the right time, somebody slow it down at least if nothing else! It was twirling like a pinwheel, that secondary hand.

Tick-tock-tick-tock-tick-tock. He broke it up into "Here I go, here I go, here I go."

There was a long period of silence that seemed to go on forever after the two of them had left. The clock told him it was only twenty-one minutes. Then at four to two a door opened above without warning—oh blessed sound, oh lovely sound!—the front door this time (over above *that* side of the basement), and high-heeled shoes clacked over his head like castanets.

"Fran!" he shouted. "Fran!" he yelled. "Fran!" he screamed. But all that got past the gag was a low whimper that didn't even reach across the basement. His face was dark with the effort it cost him, and a cord stood out at each side of his palpitating neck like a splint.

The tap-tap-tap went into the kitchen, stopped a minute (she was putting down her parcels; she didn't have things delivered because then you were expected to tip the errand-boys ten cents), came back again. If only there was something he could kick at with his interlocked feet, make a clatter with. The cellar-flooring was bare from wall to wall. He tried hoisting his lashed legs clear of the floor and pounding them down again with all his might; maybe the sound of the impact would carry up to her. All he got was a soft, cushioned sound, with twice the pain of striking a stone surface with your bare palm, and not even as much distinctness. His shoes were rubber-heeled, and he could not tilt them up and around far enough to bring them down on the leather part above the lifts. An electrical discharge of pain shot up the backs of his legs, coursed up his spine, and exploded at the back of his head, like a brilliant rocket.

Meanwhile her steps had halted about where the hall closet was (she must be hanging up her coat), then went on toward the stairs that led to the upper floor, faded out upon them, going up. She was out of earshot now, temporarily. But she was in the house with him at least! That awful aloneness was gone. He felt such gratitude for her nearness, he felt such love and need for her, he wondered how he could ever have thought of doing away with her—only one short hour ago. He saw now that he must have been insane to contemplate such a thing. Well if he had been, he was sane now, he was rational now, this ordeal had brought him to his senses. Only release him, only rescue him from his jeopardy, and he'd never again . . .

Five-after. She'd been back nine minutes now. There, it was ten. At first slowly, then faster and faster, terror,

177

which had momentarily been quelled by her return, began to fasten upon him again. Why did she stay up there on the second floor like that? Why didn't she come down here to the basement, to look for something? Wasn't there anything down here that she might suddenly be in need of? He looked around, and there wasn't. There wasn't a possible thing that might bring her down here. They kept their basement so clean, so empty. Why wasn't it piled up with all sorts of junk like other people's! That might have saved him now.

She might intend to stay up there all afternoon! She might lie down and take a nap, she might shampoo her hair, she might do over an old dress. Any one of those trivial harmless occupations of a woman during her husband's absence could prove so fatal now! She might count on staying up there until it was time to begin getting his supper ready, and if she did—no supper, no she, no he.

Then a measure of relief came again. The man. The man whom he had intended destroying along with her, *he* would save him. He would be the means of his salvation. He came other days, didn't he, in the afternoon, while Stapp was away? Then, oh God, let him come today, make this one of the days they had a rendezvous (and yet maybe it just wasn't!). For if he came, that would bring her down to the lower floor, if only to admit him. And how infinitely greater his chances would be, with two pairs of ears in the house to overhear some wisp of sound he might make, than just with one.

And so he found himself in the anomalous position of a husband praying, pleading with every ounce of fervency he can muster, for the arrival, the materialization, of a rival whose existence he had only suspected until now, never been positive of.

178

Eleven past two. Forty-nine minutes left. Less than the time it took to sit through the "A"-part of a picture-show. Less than the time it took to get a haircut, if you had to wait your turn. Less than the time it took to sit through a Sunday meal, or listen to an hour program on the radio, or ride on the bus from here to the beach for a dip. Less than all those things—to live. No, no, he had been meant to live thirty more years, forty! What had become of those years, those months, those weeks? No, not just *minutes* left, it wasn't fair!

"Fran!" he shrieked. "Fran, come down here! Can't you hear me?" The gag drank it up like a sponge.

The phone trilled out suddenly in the lower hallway, midway between him and her. He'd never heard such a beautiful sound before. "Thank God!" he sobbed, and a tear stood out in each eye. That must be the man now. That would bring her down.

Then fear again. Suppose it was only to tell her that he wasn't coming? Or worse still, suppose it was to ask her instead to come out and meet him somewhere else? Leave him alone down here, once again, with this horror ticking away opposite him. No child was ever so terrified of being left alone in the dark, of its parents putting out the light and leaving it to the mercy of the boogy-man as this grown man was at the thought of her going out of the house and leaving him behind.

It kept on ringing a moment longer, and then he heard her quick step descending the stairs to answer it. He could hear every word she said down there where he was. These cheap matchwood houses.

"Hello? Yes, Dave. I just got in now."

Then, "Oh Dave, I'm all upset. I had seventeen dollars upstairs in my bureau-drawer and it's gone, and the wristwatch that Paul gave me is gone too. Nothing else is miss-ing, but it looks to me as if someone broke in here while I was out and robbed us."

Stapp almost writhed with delight down there where he was. She knew they'd been robbed! She'd get the police now! Surely they'd search the whole place, surely they'd look down here and find him!

The man she was talking to must have asked her if she was sure. "Well, I'll look again, but I know it's gone. I know just where I left it, and it isn't there. Paul will have a fit."

No Paul wouldn't either; if she'd only come down here and free him he'd forgive her anything, even the cardinal sin of being robbed of his hard-earned money.

Then she said, "No, I haven't reported it yet. I suppose I should, but I don't like the idea—on your account, you know. I'm going to call up Paul at the shop. There's just a chance that he took the money and the watch both with him when he left this morning. I remember telling him the other night that it was losing time; he may have wanted to look it over. Well, all right, Dave; come on out then."

So he was coming, so Stapp wasn't to be left alone in the place; hot breaths of relief pushed against the sodden gag at the back of his palate.

There was a pause while she broke the connection. Then he heard her call his shop-number, "Trevelyan 4512," and wait while they were ringing, and of course no one an-swered.

Tick-tick, tick-tick, tick-tick.

The operator must have told her finally that they couldn't get the number. "Well, keep ringing," he heard her say, "it's my husband's store, he's always there at this hour."

He screamed in terrible silence: "I'm right here under

your feet! Don't waste time! For God's sake, come away from the phone, come down here!"

Finally, when failure was reported a second time, she hung up. Even the hollow, cupping sound of that detail reached him. Oh, everything reached him—but help. This was a torture that a Grand Inquisitor would have envied.

He heard her steps move away from where the phone was. Wouldn't she guess by his absence from where he was supposed to be that something was wrong? Wouldn't she come down here now and look? (Oh, where was this woman's intuition they spoke about?!) No, how could she be expected to. What connection could the basement of their house possibly have in her mind with the fact that he wasn't in his shop? She wasn't even alarmed, so far, by his absence most likely. If it had been evening; but at this hour of the day—He might have gone out later than other days to his lunch, he might have had some errand to do.

He heard her going up the stairs again, probably to resume her search for the missing money and watch. He whimpered disappointedly. He was as cut off from her, while she remained up there, as if she'd been miles away, instead of being vertically over him in a straight line.

Tick, tock, tick, tock. It was twenty-one past two now. One half-hour and nine scant minutes more left. And they ticked away with the prodigality of tropical raindrops on a corrugated tin roof.

He kept straining and pulling away from the pipe that held him fast, then falling back exhausted, to rest awhile, to struggle and to strain some more. There was as recurrent a rhythm to it as there was to the ticking of the clock itself, only more widely spaced. How could ropes hold that un-yieldingly? Each time he fell back weaker, less able to contend with them than the time before. For he wasn't little strands of hemp, he was layers of thin skin that broke one by one and gave forth burning pain and finally blood.

The doorbell rang out sharply. The man had come. In less than ten minutes after their phone talk he had reached the house. Stapp's chest started rising and falling with renewed hope. Now his chances were good again. Twice as good as before, with two people in the house instead of only one. Four ears instead of two, to hear whatever slight sound he might manage to make. And he must, he must find a way of making one. He gave the stranger his benediction while he stood there waiting to be admitted. Thank God for this admirer or whatever he was, thank God for their rendezvous. He'd give them his blessing if they wanted it, all his worldly goods; anything, anything, if they'd only find him, free him.

She came quickly down the stairs a second time and her footfalls hurried down the hall. The front door opened. "Hello, Dave," she said, and he heard the sound of a kiss quite clearly. One of those loud unabashed ones that bespeak cordiality rather than intrigue.

A man's voice, deep, resonant, asked: "Well, did it turn up yet?"

"No, and I've looked high and low," he heard her say. "I tried to get Paul after I spoke to you, and he was out to lunch."

"Well, you can't just let seventeen dollars walk out the door without lifting your finger."

For seventeen dollars they were standing there frittering his life away—and their own too, for that matter, the fools!

"They'll think I did it, I suppose," he heard the man say with a note of bitterness.

"Don't say things like that," she reproved. "Come in the kitchen and I'll make you a cup of coffee."

Her quick brittle step went first, and his heavier, slower

182

one followed. There was the sound of a couple of chairs being drawn out, and the man's footfalls died out entirely. Hers continued busily back and forth for a while, on a short orbit between stove and table.

What were they going to do, *sit* up there for the next half-hour? Couldn't he *make* them hear in some way? He tried clearing his throat, coughing. It hurt furiously, because the lining of it was all raw from long strain. But the gag muffled even the cough to a blurred purring sort of sound.

Twenty-six to three. Only minutes left now, minutes; not even a full half-hour any more.

Her footsteps stopped finally and one chair shifted slightly as she joined him at the table. There was linoleum around the stove and sink that deadened sounds, but the middle part of the room where the table stood was ordinary pine-board flooring. It let things through with crystalline accuracy.

He heard her say, "Don't you think we ought to tell Paul about—us?"

The man didn't answer for a moment. Maybe he was spooning sugar, or thinking about what she'd said. Finally he asked, "What kind of a guy is he?"

"Paul's not narrow-minded," she said. "He's very fair and broad."

Even in his agony, Stapp was dimly aware of one thing: that didn't sound a bit like her. Not her speaking well of him, but that she could calmly, detachedly contemplate broaching such a topic to him. She had always seemed so proper and slightly prudish. This argued a sophistication that he hadn't known she'd had.

The man was evidently dubious about taking Paul into their confidence, at least he had nothing further to say. She went on, as though trying to convince him: "You have

183

nothing to be afraid of on Paul's account, Dave, I know him too well. And don't you see, we can't keep on like this? It's better to go to him ourselves and tell him about you, than wait until he finds out. He's liable to think something else entirely, and keep it to himself, brood, hold it against me, unless we explain. I know that he didn't believe me that night when I helped you find a furnished room, and told him I'd been to a movie. And I'm so nervous and upset each time he comes home in the evening, it's a wonder he hasn't noticed it before now. Why I feel as guilty as if—as if I were one of these disloyal wives or something." She laughed embarrassedly, as if apologizing to him for even bringing such a comparison up.

What did she mean by that?

"Didn't you ever tell him about me at all?"

"You mean in the beginning? Oh, I told him you'd been in one or two scrapes, but like a little fool I let him think I'd lost track of you, didn't know where you were any more."

Why, that was her brother she'd said that about!

The man sitting up there with her confirmed it right as the thought burst in his mind. "I know it's tough on you, Sis. You're happily married and all that. I've got no right to come around and gum things up for you. No one's proud of a jailbird, an escaped convict, for a brother—"

"David," he heard her say, and even through the flooring there was such a ring of earnestness in her voice Stapp could almost visualize her reaching across the table and putting her hand reassuringly on his, "there isn't anything I wouldn't do for you, and you should know that by now. Circumstances have been against you, that's all. You shouldn't have done what you did, but that's spilt milk and there's no use going back over it now."

"I suppose I'll have to go back and finish it out. Seven years, though, Fran, seven years out of a man's life—"

"But this way you have no life at all—"

Were they going to keep on talking his life away? Nineteen to three. One quarter of an hour, and four minutes over!

"Before you do anything, let's go downtown and talk it over with Paul, hear what he says." One chair jarred back, then the other. He could hear dishes clatter, as though they'd all been lumped together in one stack. "I'll do these when I come back," she remarked.

Were they going to leave again? Were they going to leave him behind here, alone, with only minutes to spare?

Their footsteps had come out into the hall now, halted a moment undecidedly. "I don't like the idea of you being seen with me on the streets in broad daylight, you could get in trouble yourself, you know. Why don't you phone him to come out here instead?"

Yes, yes, Stapp wailed. Stay with me! Stay!

"I'm not afraid," she said gallantly. "I don't like to ask him to leave his work at this hour, and I can't tell him over the phone. Wait a minute, I'll get my hat." Her footsteps diverged momentarily from his, rejoined them again.

Panic-stricken, Stapp did the only thing he could think of. Struck the back of his head violently against the thick pipe he was attached to.

A sheet of blue flame darted before his eyes. He must have hit one of the welts where he had already been struck once by the burglars. The pain was so excruciating he knew he couldn't repeat the attempt. But they must have heard something, some dull thud or reverberation must have carried up along the pipe. He heard her stop short for a minute and say, "What was that?"

And the man, duller-sensed than she and killing him all unknowingly, "What? I didn't hear anything."

She took his word for it, went on again, to the hall-closet

185

to get her coat. Then her footsteps retraced themselves all the way back through the dining-room to the kitchen. "Wait a minute, I want to make sure this back door's shut tight. Locking the stable after the horse is gone!"

She came forward again through the house for the last time, there was the sound of the front door opening, she passed through it, the man passed through it, it closed, and they were gone. There was the faint whirr of a car starting up outside in the open.

And now he was left alone with his self-fashioned doom a second time, and the first seemed a paradise in retrospect compared to this, for then he had a full hour to spare, he had been rich in time, and now he only had fifteen minutes, one miserly quarter-hour.

There wasn't any use struggling any more. He'd found that out long ago. He couldn't anyway, even if he'd wanted to. Flames seemed to be licking lazily around his wrists and ankles.

He'd found a sort of palliative now, the only way there was left. He'd keep his eyes down and pretend the hands were moving slower than they were, it was better than watching them constantly, it blunted a little of the terror at least. The ticking he couldn't hide from. Of course every once in a while when he couldn't resist looking up and verifying his own calculations, there'd be a renewed burst of anguish, but in-between-times it made it more bearable to say, "It's only gained a half-minute since the last time I looked." Then he'd hold out as long as he could with his eyes down, but when he couldn't stand it any more and would have to raise them to see if he was right, it had gained *two* minutes. Then he'd have a bad fit of hysterics, in which he called on God, and even on his long-dead mother, to help him, and couldn't see straight through the tears. Then he'd pull himself together again, in a measure, and start the self-deception over again. "It's only about thirty seconds now since I last looked. . . . Now it's about a minute . . ." (But was it? But was it?) And so on, mounting slowly to another climax of terror and abysmal collapse.

Then suddenly the outside world intruded again, that world that he was so cut off from that it already seemed as far-away, as unreal, as if he were already dead. The doorbell rang out.

He took no hope from the summons at first. Maybe some peddler—no, that had been too aggressive to be a peddler's ring. It was the sort of ring that claimed admission as its right, not as a favor. It came again. Whoever was ringing was truculently impatient at being kept waiting. A third ring was given the bell, this time a veritable blast that kept on for nearly half-a-minute. The party must have kept his finger pressed to the bell-button the whole time. Then as the peal finally stopped, a voice called out forcefully: "Anybody home in there? Gas Company!" And suddenly Stapp was quivering all over, almost whinnying in his anxiety.

This was the one call, the one incident in all the day's domestic routine, from earliest morning until latest night, that could have possibly brought anyone down into the basement! The meter was up there on the wall, beside the stairs, staring him in the face! And her brother had had to take her out of the house at just this particular time! There was no one to let the man in.

There was the impatient shuffle of a pair of feet on the cement walk. The man must have come down off the porch to gain perspective with which to look inquiringly up at the second-floor windows. And for a fleeting moment, as he chafed and shifted about out there before the house, on the walk and off, Stapp actually glimpsed the blurred shanks of his legs standing before the grimy transom that let light into the basement at ground-level. All the potential savior had to do was crouch down and peer in through it, and he'd see him tied up down there. And the rest would be so easy!

Why didn't he, why didn't he? But evidently he didn't expect anyone to be in the basement of a house in which his triple ring went unanswered. The tantalizing trouser-leg shifted out of range again, the transom became blank. A little saliva filtered through the mass of rag in Stapp's distended mouth, trickled across his silently vibrating lower lip.

The gas inspector gave the bell one more try, as if venting his disappointment at being balked rather than in any expectation of being admitted this late in the proceedings. He gave it innumerable short jabs, like a telegraph-key. Bip-bip-bip-bip-bip. Then he called out disgustedly, evidently for the benefit of some unseen assistant waiting in a truck out at the curb, "They're never in when you want 'em to be!" There was a single quick tread on the cement, away from the house. Then the slur of a light truck being driven off.

Stapp died a little. Not metaphorically, literally. His arms and legs got cold up to the elbows and knees, his heart seemed to beat slower, and he had trouble getting a full breath; more saliva escaped and ran down his chin, and his head drooped forward and lay on his chest for awhile, inert.

Tick-tick, tick-tick, tick-tick. It brought him to after awhile, as though it were something beneficent, smelling salts or ammonia, instead of being the malevolent thing it was.

He noticed that his mind was starting to wander. Not much, as yet, but every once in awhile he'd get strange fancies. One time he thought that his *face* was the clock-dial, and that thing he kept staring at over there was his face. The pivot in the middle that held the two hands became his nose, and the 10 and the 2, up near the top, became his eyes, and he had a red-tin beard and head of hair and a little round bell on the exact top of his crown for a hat. "Gee, I look funny," he sobbed drowsily. And he caught himself twitching the muscles of his face, as if trying to stop those two hands that were clasped on it before they progressed any further and killed that man over there, who was breathing so metallically: tick, tock, tick, tock.

Then he drove the weird notion away again, and he saw that it had been just another escape-mechanism. Since he couldn't control the clock over there, he had attempted to change it into something else. Another vagary was that this ordeal had been brought on him as punishment for what he had intended doing to Fran, that he was being held fast there not by the inanimate ropes but by some active, punitive agency, and that if he exhibited remorse, pledged contrition to a proper degree, he could automatically effect his release at its hands. Thus over and over he whined in the silence of his throttled throat, "I'm sorry. I won't do it again. Just let me go this one time, I've learned my lesson, I'll never do it again."

The outer world returned again. This time it was the phone. It must be Fran and her brother, trying to find out if he'd come back here in their absence. They'd found the shop closed, must have waited outside of it for a while, and then when he still didn't come, didn't know what to make of it. Now they were calling the house from a booth down there, to see if he had been taken ill, had returned here in the meantime. When no one answered, that would tell them, surely, that something was wrong. Wouldn't they come back now to find out what had happened to him?

But why should they think he was here in the house if he didn't answer the phone? How could they dream he was in the basement the whole time? They'd hang around out-side the shop some more waiting for him, until as time went on, and Fran became real worried, maybe they'd go to the police. (But that would be hours from now, what good would it do?) They'd look everywhere but here for him. When a man is reported missing the last place they'd look for him would be in his own home.

It stopped ringing finally, and its last vibration seemed to hang tenuously on the lifeless air long after it had ceased, humming outward in a spreading circle like a pebble dropped into a stagnant pool. *Mmmmmmmmm*, until it was gone, and silence came rolling back in its wake.

She would be outside the pay-booth or wherever it was she had called from, by this time. Rejoining her brother, where he had waited. Reporting, "He's not out at the house either." Adding the mild, still unworried comment, "Isn't that strange? Where on earth can he have gone?" Then they'd go back and wait outside the locked shop, at ease, secure, unendangered. She'd tap her foot occasionally in slight impatience, look up and down the street while they chatted.

And now *they* would be two of those casuals who would stop short and say to one another at three o'clock: "What was that?" And Fran might add, "It sounded as though it came from out our way." That would be the sum-total of their comment on his passing.

Tick, tock, tick, tock, tick, tock. Nine minutes to three. Oh, what a lovely number was nine. Let it be nine forever, not eight or seven, nine for all eternity. Make time stand still, that he might breathe though all the world around him stagnated, rotted away. But no, it was already eight. The hand had bridged the white gap between the two black notches. Oh, what a precious number was eight, so rounded, so symmetrical. Let it be eight forever—

A woman's voice called out in sharp reprimand, some-where outside in the open: "Be careful what you're doing, Bobby, you'll break a window!" She was some distance away, but the ringing dictatorial tones carried clearly.

Stapp saw the blurred shape of a ball strike the base-ment-transom, he was looking up at it, for her voice had come in to him through there. It must have been just a tennis-ball, but for an instant it was outlined black against the soiled pane, like a small cannonball; it seemed to hang there suspended, to adhere to the glass, then it dropped back to the ground. If it had been ordinary glass it might have broken it, but the wire-mesh had prevented that.

The child came close up against the transom to get its ball back. It was such a small child that Stapp could see its entire body within the height of the pane, only the head was cut off. It bent over to pick up the ball, and then its head came into range too. It had short golden ringlets all over it. Its profile was turned toward him, looking down at the ball. It was the first human face he'd seen since he'd been left where he was. It looked like an angel. But an inattentive, unconcerned angel.

It saw something else while it was still bent forward close to the ground, a stone or something that attracted it, and picked that up too and looked at it, still crouched over, then finally threw it recklessly away over its shoulder, whatever it was.

The woman's voice was nearer at hand now, she must be strolling along the sidewalk directly in front of the house. "Bobby, stop throwing things like that, you'll hit some-body!"

If it would only turn its head over this way, it could look right in, it could see him. The glass wasn't too smeary for that. He started to weave his head violently from side to side, hoping the flurry of motion would attract it, catch its eye. It may have, or its own natural curiosity may have prompted it to look in without that. Suddenly it had turned its head and was looking directly in through the transom. Blankly at first, he could tell by the vacant expression of its eyes.

Faster and faster he swiveled his head. It raised the heel of one chubby, fumbling hand and scoured a little clear spot to squint through. Now it could see him, now surely! It still didn't for a second. It must be much darker in here than outside, and the light was behind it.

The woman's voice came in sharp reproof: "Bobby, what are you doing there?!"

And then suddenly it saw him. The pupils of its eyes shifted over a little, came to rest directly on him. Interest replaced blankness. Nothing is strange to children—not a man tied up in a cellar any more than anything else—yet everything is. Everything creates wonder, calls for comment, demands explanation. Wouldn't it say anything to her? Couldn't it talk? It must be old enough to; she, its mother, was talking to it incessantly. "Bobby, come away from there!"

"Mommy, look!" it said gleefully.

Stapp couldn't see it clearly any more, he was shaking his head so fast. He was dizzy, like you are when you've just gotten off a carousel; the transom and the child it framed kept swinging about him in a half-circle, first too far over on one side, then too far over on the other.

But wouldn't it understand, wouldn't it understand that weaving of the head meant he wanted to be free? Even if ropes about the wrists and ankles had no meaning to it, if it couldn't tell what a bandage around the mouth was, it must know that when anyone writhed like that they wanted to be let loose. Oh God, if it had only been two years older, three at the most! A child of eight, these days, would have understood and given warning.

"Bobby, are you coming? I'm waiting!"

If he could only hold its attention, keep it rooted there long enough in disobedience to her, surely she'd come over and get it, see him herself as she irritably sought to ascertain the reason for its fascination.

He rolled his eyes at it in desperate comicality, winked them, blinked them, crossed them. An elfin grin peered out on its face at this last; already it found humor in a physical defect, or the assumption of one, young as it was.

An adult hand suddenly darted downward from the upper right-hand corner of the transom, caught its wrist, bore its arm upward out of sight. "Mommy, look!" it said again, and pointed with its other hand. "Funny man, tied up."

The adult voice, reasonable, logical, dispassionate—inattentive to a child's fibs and fancies—answered: "Why that wouldn't look nice, Mommy can't peep into other people's houses like you can."

The child was tugged erect at the end of its arm, its head disappeared above the transom. Its body was pivoted around, away from him; he could see the hollows at the back of its knees for an instant longer, then its outline on the glass blurred in withdrawal, it was gone. Only the little clear spot it had scoured remained to mock him in his crucifixion.

The will to live is an unconquerable thing. He was more dead than alive by now, yet presently he started to crawl back again out of the depths of his despair, a slower longer crawl each time, like that of some indefatigable insect buried repeatedly in sand, that each time manages to burrow its way out.

He rolled his head away from the window back toward

the clock finally. He hadn't been able to spare a look at it during the whole time the child was in sight. And now to his horror it stood at three to three. There was a fresh, a final blotting-out of the burrowing insect that was his hopes, as if by a cruel idler lounging on a beach.

He couldn't *feel* any more, terror or hope or anything else. A sort of numbness had set in, with a core of gleaming awareness remaining that was his mind. *That* would be all that the detonation would be able to blot out by the time it came. It was like having a tooth extracted with the aid of novocaine. There remained of him now only this single pulsing nerve of premonition; all the tissue around it was frozen. So protracted foreknowledge of death was in itself its own anaesthetic.

Now it would be too late even to attempt to free him first, before stopping the thing. Just time enough, if someone came down those stairs this very minute, sharp-edged knife with which to sever his bonds already in hand, for him to throw himself over toward it, reverse it. And now —now it was too late even for that, too late for anything but to die.

He was making animal-noises deep in his throat as the minute hand slowly blended with the notch of twelve. Guttural sounds like a dog worrying a bone, though the gag prevented their emerging in full volume. He puckered the flesh around his eyes apprehensively, creased them into slits—as though the closing of his eyes could ward off, lessen, the terrific force of what was to come! Something deep within him, what it was he had no leisure nor skill to recognize, seemed to retreat down long dim corridors away from the doom that impeded. He hadn't known he had those convenient corridors of evasion in him, with their protective turns and angles by which to put distance between himself and menace. Oh clever architect of the Mind, oh merciful blueprints that made such emergency exits available. Toward them this something, that was he and yet not he, rushed; toward sanctuary, security, toward waiting brightness, sunshine, laughter.

The hand on the dial stayed there, upright, perpendicular, a perfect right-angle to its corollary, while the swift seconds that were all there were left of existence ticked by and were gone. It wasn't so straight now any more, but he didn't know it, he was in a state of death already. White reappeared between it and the twelve-notch, *behind* it now. It was one minute after three. He was shaking all over from head to foot—not with fear, with laughter.

It broke into sound as they plucked the dampened, bloodied gag out, as though they were drawing the laughter out after it, by suction or osmosis.

"No, don't take those ropes off him yet!" the man in the white coat warned the policeman sharply. "Wait'll they get here with the straitjacket first, or you'll have your hands full."

Fran said through her tears, cupping her hands to her ears, "Can't you stop him from laughing like that? I can't stand it. Why does he keep laughing like that?"

"He's out of his mind, lady," explained the intern patiently.

The clock said five past seven. "What's in this box?" the cop asked, kicking at it idly with his foot. It shifted lightly along the wall a little, and took the clock with it.

"Nothing," Stapp's wife answered, through her sobs and above his incessant laughter. "Just an empty box. It used to have some kind of fertilizer in it, but I took it out and used it on the flowers I—I've been trying to raise out in back of the house."

Inflexible Logic

Russell Maloney

Russell Maloney wrote articles and short stories for The New Yorker *fifty years ago. His pieces, at their best, are funny in a very odd and individual way.*

In this brief classic, he takes the old chestnut about the six monkeys at typewriters and turns it into one of the strangest and funniest stories I know anything about.

It does have a crime in it—two, in fact, at the least —and that provides enough excuse for including it here. It shouldn't be missed by any reader.

When the six chimpanzees came into his life, Mr. Bainbridge was thirty-eight years old. He was a bachelor and lived comfortably in a remote part of Connecticut, in a large old house with a carriage drive, a conservatory, a tennis court, and a well-selected library. His income was derived from impeccably situated real estate in New York City, and he spent it soberly, in a manner which could give offence to nobody. Once a year, late in April, his tennis court was resurfaced, and after that anybody in the neighborhood was welcome to use it; his monthly statement from Brentano's seldom ran below seventy-five dollars; every third year, in November, he turned in his old Cadillac coupé for a new one; he ordered his cigars, which were mild and rather moderately priced, in shipments of one thousand, from a tobacconist in Havana; because of the international situation he had cancelled arrangements to travel abroad, and after due thought had decided to spend his travelling allowance on wines, which seemed likely to get scarcer and more expensive if the war lasted. On the whole, Mr. Bainbridge's life was deliberately, and not too unsuccessfully, modelled after that of an English country gentleman of the late eighteenth century, a gentleman interested in the arts and in the expansion of science, and so sure of himself that he didn't care if some people thought him eccentric.

Mr. Bainbridge had many friends in New York, and he spent several days of the month in the city, staying at his club and looking around. Sometimes he called up a girl and took her out to a theatre and a night club. Sometimes he and a couple of classmates got a little tight and went to a prizefight. Mr. Bainbridge also looked in now and then at some of the conservative art galleries, and liked occasionally to go to a concert. And he liked cocktail parties, too, because of the fine footling conversation and the extraordinary number of pretty girls who had nothing else to do with the rest of their evening. It was at a New York cocktail party, however, that Mr. Bainbridge kept his preliminary appointment with doom. At one of the parties given by Hobie Packard, the stockbroker, he learned about the theory of the six chimpanzees.

It was almost six-forty. The people who had intended to have one drink and go had already gone, and the people who intended to stay were fortifying themselves with slightly dried canapés and talking animatedly. A group of stage and radio people had coagulated in one corner, near Packard's Capehart, and were wrangling about various methods of cheating the Collector of Internal Revenue. In another corner was a group of stockbrokers, talking about the greatest stockbroker of them all, Gauguin. Little Marcia Lupton was sitting with a young man, saying earnestly, "Do you really want to know what my greatest ambition is? I want to be myself," and Mr. Bainbridge smiled gently, thinking of the time Marcia had said that to him. Then he heard the voice of Bernard Weiss, the critic, saying, "Of course he wrote one good novel. It's not surprising. After all, we know that if six chimpanzees were set to work pounding six typewriters at random, they would, in a million years, write all the books in the British Museum."

Mr. Bainbridge drifted over to Weiss and was introduced to Weiss's companion, a Mr. Noble. "What's this about a million chimpanzees, Weiss?" he asked.

"Six chimpanzees," Mr. Weiss said. "It's an old cliché of the mathematicians. I thought everybody was told about it in school. Law of averages, you know, or maybe it's permutation and combination. The six chimps, just pounding away at the typewriter keys, would be bound to copy out all the books ever written by man. There are only so many possible combinations of letters and numerals, and they'd produce all of them—see? Of course they'd also turn out a mountain of gibberish, but they'd work the books in, too. All the books in the British Museum."

Mr. Bainbridge was delighted; this was the sort of talk he liked to hear when he came to New York. "Well, but look here," he said, just to keep up his part in the foolish conversation, "what if one of the chimpanzees finally did duplicate a book, right down to the last period, but left that off? Would that count?"

"I suppose not. Probably the chimpanzee would get around to doing the book again, and put the period in."

"What nonsense!" Mr. Noble cried.

"It may be nonsense, but Sir James Jeans believes it," Mr. Weiss said, huffily. "Jeans or Lancelot Hogben. I know I ran across it quite recently."

Mr. Bainbridge was impressed. He read quite a bit of popular science, and both Jeans and Hogben were in his library. "Is that so?" he murmured, no longer feeling frivolous. "Wonder if it has ever actually been tried? I mean, has anybody ever put six chimpanzees in a room with six typewriters and a lot of paper?"

Mr. Weiss glanced at Mr. Bainbridge's empty cocktail glass and said drily, "Probably not."

Nine weeks later, on a winter evening, Mr. Bainbridge was sitting in his study with his friend James Mallard, an assistant professor of mathematics at New Haven. He was plainly nervous as he poured himself a drink and said, "Mallard, I've asked you to come here—Brandy? Cigar? —for a particular reason. You remember that I wrote you some time ago, asking your opinion of . . . of a certain mathematical hypothesis or supposition."

"Yes," Professor Mallard said, briskly. "I remember perfectly. About the six chimpanzees and the British Museum. And I told you it was a perfectly sound popularization of a principle known to every schoolboy who had studied the science of probabilities."

"Precisely," Mr. Bainbridge said. "Well, Mallard, I made up my mind. . . . It was not difficult for me, because I have, in spite of that fellow in the White House, been able to give something every year to the Museum of Natural History, and they were naturally glad to oblige me. . . . And after all, the only contribution a layman can make to the progress of science is to assist with the drudgery of experiment. . . . In short, I—"

"I suppose you're trying to tell me that you have procured six chimpanzees and set them to work at typewriters in order to see whether they will eventually write all the books in the British Museum. Is that it?"

"Yes, that's it," Mr. Bainbridge said. "What a mind you have, Mallard. Six fine young males, in perfect condition. I had a—I suppose you'd call it a dormitory—built out in back of the stable. The typewriters are in the conservatory. It's light and airy in there, and I moved most of the plants out. Mr. North, the man who owns the circus, very obligingly let me engage one of his best animal men. Really, it was no trouble at all."

Professor Mallard smiled indulgently. "After all, such a thing is not unheard of," he said. "I seem to remember that a man at some university put his graduate students to work flipping coins, to see if heads and tails came up an equal number of times. Of course they did."

Mr. Bainbridge looked at his friend very queerly. "Then you believe that any such principle of the science of probabilities will stand up under an actual test?"

"Certainly."

"You had better see for yourself." Mr. Bainbridge led Professor Mallard downstairs, along a corridor, through a disused music room, and into a large conservatory. The middle of the floor had been cleared of plants and was occupied by a row of six typewriter tables, each one supporting a hooded machine. At the left of each typewriter was a neat stack of yellow copy paper. Empty wastebaskets were under each table. The chairs were the unpadded, spring-backed kind favored by experienced stenographers. A large bunch of ripe bananas was hanging in one corner, and in another stood a Great Bear water-cooler and a rack of Lily cups. Six piles of typescript, each about a foot high, were ranged along the wall on an improvised shelf. Mr. Bainbridge picked up one of the piles, which he could just conveniently lift, and set it on a table before Professor Mallard. "The output to date of Chimpanzee A, known as Bill," he said simply.

" 'Oliver Twist, by Charles Dickens,' " Professor Mallard read out. He read the first and second pages of the manuscript, then feverishly leafed through to the end. "You mean to tell me," he said, "that this chimpanzee has written—"

"Word for word and comma for comma," said Mr. Bainbridge. "Young, my butler, and I took turns comparing it with the edition I own. Having finished Oliver Twist, Bill is, as you see, starting the sociological works of Vilfredo Pareto, in Italian. At the rate he has been going, it should keep him busy for the rest of the month."

"And all the chimpanzees"—Professor Mallard was pale, and enunciated with difficulty—"they aren't all—"

"Oh, yes, all writing books which I have every reason to believe are in the British Museum. The prose of John Donne, some Anatole France, Conan Doyle, Galen, the collected plays of Somerset Maugham, Marcel Proust, the memoirs of the late Marie of Rumania, and a monograph by u Dr. Wiley on the marsh grasses of Maine and Massachusetts. I can sum it up for you, Mallard, by telling you that since I started this experiment, four weeks and some days ago, none of the chimpanzees has spoiled a single sheet of paper."

Professor Mallard straightened up, passed his handkerchief across his brow, and took a deep breath. "I apologize for my weakness," he said. "It was simply the sudden shock. No, looking at the thing scientifically—and I hope I am at least as capable of that as the next man—there is nothing marvellous about the situation. These chimpanzees, or a succession of similar teams of chimpanzees, would in a million years write all the books in the British Museum. I told you some time ago that I believed that statement. Why should my belief be altered by the fact that they produced some of the books at the very outset? After all, I should not be very much surprised if I tossed a coin a hundred times and it came up heads every time. I know that if I kept at it long enough, the ratio would reduce itself to an exact fifty per cent. Rest assured, these chimpanzees will begin to compose gibberish quite soon. It is bound to happen. Science tells us so. Meanwhile, I advise you to keep this experiment secret. Uninformed people might create a sensation if they knew."

"I will, indeed," Mr. Bainbridge said. "And I'm very grateful for your rational analysis. It reassures me. And now, before you go, you must hear the new Schnabel records that arrived today."

During the succeeding three months, Professor Mallard got into the habit of telephoning Mr. Bainbridge every Friday afternoon at five-thirty, immediately after leaving his seminar room. The Professor would say, "Well?," and Mr. Bainbridge would reply, "They're still at it, Mallard. Haven't spoiled a sheet of paper yet." If Mr. Bainbridge had to go out on Friday afternoon, he would leave a written message with his butler, who would read it to Professor Mallard: "Mr. Bainbridge says we now have Trevelyan's *Life of Macaulay*, the *Confessions of Saint Augustine*, *Vanity Fair*, part of Irving's *Life of George Washington*, the *Book of the Dead*, and some speeches delivered in Parliament in opposition to the Corn Laws, sir." Professor Mallard would reply, with a hint of a snarl in his voice, "Tell him to remember what I predicted," and hang up with a clash.

The eleventh Friday that Professor Mallard telephoned, Mr. Bainbridge said, "No change. I have had to store the bulk of the manuscript in the cellar. I would have burned it, except that it probably has some scientific value."

"How dare you talk of scientific value?" The voice from New Haven roared faintly in the receiver. "Scientific value! You—you—chimpanzee!" There were further inarticulate sputterings, and Mr. Bainbridge hung up with a disturbed expression. "I am afraid Mallard is overtaxing himself," he murmured.

Next day, however, he was pleasantly surprised. He was leafing through a manuscript that had been completed the previous day by Chimpanzee D, Corky. It was the complete diary of Samuel Pepys, and Mr. Bainbridge was chuckling over the naughty passages, which were omitted in his own edition, when Professor Mallard was shown into the room. "I have come to apologize for my outrageous conduct on the telephone yesterday," the Professor said.

"Please don't think of it any more. I know you have many things on your mind," Mr. Bainbridge said. "Would you like a drink?"

"A large whiskey, straight, please," Professor Mallard said. "I got rather cold driving down. No change, I presume?"

"No, none. Chimpanzee F, Dinty, is just finishing John Florio's translation of Montaigne's essays, but there is no other news of interest."

Professor Mallard squared his shoulders and tossed off his drink in one astonishing gulp. "I should like to see them at work," he said. "Would I disturb them, do you think?"

"Not at all. As a matter of fact, I usually look in on them around this time of day. Dinty may have finished his Montaigne by now, and it is always interesting to see them start a new work. I would have thought that they would continue on the same sheet of paper, but they don't, you know. Always a fresh sheet, and the title in capitals."

Professor Mallard, without apology, poured another drink and slugged it down. "Lead on," he said.

It was dusk in the conservatory, and the chimpanzees were typing by the light of student lamps clamped to their desks. The keeper lounged in a corner, eating a banana and reading *Billboard*. "You might as well take an hour or so off," Mr. Bainbridge said. The man left.

Professor Mallard, who had not taken off his overcoat, stood with his hands in his pockets, looking at the busy

205

chimpanzees. "I wonder if you know, Bainbridge, that the science of probabilities takes everything into account," he said, in a queer, tight voice. "It is certainly almost beyond the bounds of credibility that these chimpanzees should write books without a single error, but that abnormality may be corrected by—*these!*" He took his hands from his pockets, and each one held a .38 revolver. "Stand back out of harm's way!" he shouted.

"Mallard! Stop it!" The revolvers barked, first the right hand, then the left, then the right. Two chimpanzees fell, and a third reeled into a corner. Mr. Bainbridge seized his friend's arm and wrested one of the weapons from him.

"Now I am armed, too, Mallard, and I advise you to stop!" he cried. Professor Mallard's answer was to draw a bead on Chimpanzee E and shoot him dead. Mr. Bainbridge made a rush, and Professor Mallard fired at him. Mr. Bainbridge, in his quick death agony, tightened his finger on the trigger of his revolver. It went off, and Professor Mallard went down. On his hands and knees he fired at the two chimpanzees which were still unhurt, and then collapsed.

There was nobody to hear his last words. "The human equation . . . always the enemy of science . . ." he panted. "This time . . . vice versa . . . I, a mere mortal . . . savior of science . . . deserve a Nobel . . ."

When the old butler came running into the conservatory to investigate the noises, his eyes were met by a truly appalling sight. The student lamps were shattered, but a newly risen moon shone in through the conservatory windows on the corpses of the two gentlemen, each clutching a smoking revolver. Five of the chimpanzees were dead. The sixth was Chimpanzee F. His right arm disabled, obviously bleeding to death, he was slumped before his typewriter. Painfully, with his left hand, he took from the machine the completed last page of Florio's Montaigne. Groping for a fresh sheet, he inserted it, and typed with one finger, "UNCLE TOM'S CABIN, by Harriet Beecher Stowe. Chapte . . ." Then he, too, was dead.